Face-Off

Cord's arms were pinioned. He could feel his ribs crushed to the breaking point. Bearclaws had the upper half of Cord's body bent backward so he had no leverage for a kick to the balls. Cord pulled his head forward, moving close to Bearclaws' face as if he intended to give the mountain man a kiss. Cord opened his mouth wide and snapped his teeth down hard on Bearclaws' nose. He felt his teeth crunching through cartilage and bone. His mouth tasted salty from Bearclaws' blood. As he pulled his head away he heard the soft tear of flesh as his teeth still clenched on the mountain man's nostrils. He spit out chunks of skin and bits of cartilage as the mountain man's thick blood dribbled down his chin.

Bearclaws screamed in agony. He dropped Cord, moving his hands up to his face.

"That Diamondback is giving old Bearclaws some trouble," Amanda Applegate observed.

Also by Pike Bishop:

DIAMONDBACK
DIAMONDBACK #2:
    JUDGEMENT AT POISONED WELL

DIAMONDBACK #3

SNAKE EYES
by PIKE BISHOP

PINNACLE BOOKS   NEW YORK

An acknowledgment is made to the contributions of Gene Garofalo for his assistance on this book.

DIAMONDBACK #3: SNAKE EYES

An original Pinnacle Books edition, published for the first time anywhere.

First printing, February 1984

ISBN: 0-523-42147-8

Can. ISBN: 0-523-43134-1

Cover illustration by Aleta Jenks

Printed in the United States of America

PINNACLE BOOKS, INC.
1430 Broadway
New York, New York 10018

9 8 7 6 5 4 3 2 1

SNAKE EYES

1

"Diamondback!" Bearclaws Boone roared. "What kind of name is that? Sounds Injun to me. Hey, barkeep! You servin redskins now?"

Cord Diamondback kept his black eyes straight ahead, staring placidly at a faded and peeling poster of Buffalo Bill's Wild West Congress. He casually rested his lukewarm beer on the bar. The Glory Hole saloon seemed a typical whiskey mill. Wooden planks covering empty nail kegs made up the serving area. A red-hot potbelly stove warmed one corner of the room where most of the patrons congregated. Cord's boots sunk in the inch-high sawdust covering the green-lumber floor. Every one of these places seemed to have a resident bully anxious to pick a fight with a stranger. Cord usually ignored them. He couldn't make a profit from a barroom brawl.

There was something about Cord's appearance

that captured the interest of both men and women. His size was not imposing, although his slim body bristled with tight muscles that looked terribly efficient. His features were handsome in a rough-hewn, angular way, but his face was not the reason he stood out. It was the way Cord carried himself, not cocky, but in a manner that demanded respect. Women suspected that something dangerous and barely controlled, like hornets in an uncorked bottle, might lie under his impassive exterior. The idea excited them. Men usually treated him carefully, but occasionally a man would look at Cord and feel challenged. Not because of anything he had said or done, but because he was *there* and he seemed so self-assured.

Boone's half-full whiskey bottle was clutched in his hairy paw. His throat rippled as he drank from the bottle, his gray-streaked beard so thick the whiskey appeared to be disappearing into a moldy nest. "I come to town once a year and I'd admire doing my drinking in a place that don't carry the stench of Injun." Boone carried his complaint to the saloon at large as if Cord weren't present.

Cord kept silent while Boone ranted. He lifted his beer with his left hand and casually lowered the right near the holster of his Smith and Wesson Schofield .44. His hips shifted imperceptibly to balance his body weight. He didn't want a scrap, particularly with a judging job close at hand. But he was ready.

He's obviously not a townsman, Cord thought, inspecting the loudmouth out of the corner of his eye. Folks appeared more civilized even in a desolate one-street town like Crestview. Bearclaws looked like something you'd find in your trap. Something like a rabid wolverine that was going to give you more trouble than the pelt was worth.

Bearclaws wore a buckskin shirt and leggings. Both were decorated with the remnants of beads and porcupine quills. The outfit seemed fifty years out of date. Cord didn't see much buckskin anymore, except on dudes who wanted to dress like real westerners. Boone obviously wasn't trying to impress anyone. Cord could tell by the rotten smell as if he hadn't scraped away all the flesh when skinning the deer.

"Don't nobody care about the stink of that Injun but me?" Bearclaws asked. The men standing close to Cord melted away from him as if they'd heard he was carrying cholera.

Boone stood a few inches shorter than Cord's six feet, but he seemed twice as wide. His broad, barrel chest nearly burst from the buckskin shirt and his muscular shoulders seemed to flow in a straight line to his untapered waist. His body looked like a solid slab of carved rock, similar to the monoliths Cord had seen on Easter Island during his whaling days.

"Ain't you gonna say nothing?" Bearclaws demanded. He stood facing Cord in a direct confrontation.

"Don't want no trouble in here," the bartender told Bearclaws in an apologetic tone. He was a little man with a paunch that threatened to knock over the two-by-fours that served as the bar.

When his resources ran low, Cord occasionally fought for prizes. He rated Bearclaws as a potential opponent. The son of a bitch was bulky, probably weighing a good one hundred pounds over Cord's trim one seventy-five. Cord was impressed by Bearclaws' abnormally long arms that dangled just below his knees. Cord admitted to himself that he wouldn't want to be caught up in those arms. A bear hug from Bearclaws could crush a man's chest. Strong, compact, low center of gravity and Neanderthal arms; he might be more than I can handle, Cord thought. Another good reason to avoid a fight.

Boone's presence completely sobered the men in the Glory Hole. Some chawed silently and spat sticky tobacco juice into the sawdust, where it lay in little gobules. Others downed their whiskey in long gulps that only sobered them some more.

Cord studied Buffalo Bill's poster more closely and read that the Congress featured real Wild West Indians. Thrilling, Cord thought. I'd see the show, but it might be more excitement than I can stand.

"I was wrong," Bearclaws muttered. He eyed Cord contemptously. "You ain't no Injun, you're a chicken. Hey, maybe you're a Rhode Island red." His eyes scanned the room as if he expected a laugh. The men in the saloon were silent. "This place is like a church," Bearclaws snorted, "except I never seen a church with no chicken Injuns in it." He threw up his arms in disgust.

Bearclaws started for the swinging doors glaring a challenge at every man present. He stopped near the entrance and fastened his eyes on Cord. "I'm goin' outside to take a piss. When I come back, I'm goin' find out if this chicken can lay eggs."

A middle-aged man with a pockmarked face that looked like a miniature gravel pit watched the proceedings with some amusement. "One peep out of you and he'd have bit your head off," he told Cord. He extended a slim hand toward Cord. "I'm Will Kincaid, town barber. If I was you, I'd be gone by the time he gets back."

"Who is this Bearclaws?" Cord asked.

"He's our mountain man," Kincaid answered with a tooth-missing grin that made him look like a jack-o'-lantern with the candle snuffed out. "Old Bearclaws drifts down from the high Rockies once a year to trade for provisions."

A mountain man! There were damn few of the back-country hermits left. The market for beaver pelts disappeared long ago when silk hats replaced felt in eastern fashion. The pelts used to be called "hairy bank notes." When they became worthless, only misfits still lived where the land was so hostile.

"I guess you want to hear more about the man," the bartender said, eyeing Cord's beer glass with anticipation.

"Don't wait to hear about nothin'," Kincaid cautioned. "You'd best skedaddle out of here. Boone said he's coming back."

Cord set down his beer glass. "Your eloquence convinced me," he said. "I'm leaving."

Cord didn't want to be caught in a mindless fistfight while waiting for his contact. Word had reached him through one of his usual sources that he was wanted for a judging job in Crestview. He had a reputation for settling disputes that couldn't be handled by the courts. The anonymous message contained a five-hundred-dollar advance and the cryptic note to the effect that the future of Colorado would be shaped by his decision. Cord was more interested in his own future. He'd come to learn more because the message promised ten times the amount of the advance once the job was completed. Five thousand dollars was a good enough reason to ride to Crestview.

"Bearclaws'll fight anything on two or four legs," the bartender called after Cord, unwilling to let his audience leave.

"That's one animal or two men," Kincaid interjected. The bartender glared at the interruption.

Cord was near the door now. He turned toward the two men and smiled. "Sounds like you folks are grateful for the excitement." He noticed the bartender was staring past him. Kincaid was looking in the same direction.

"I'm looking for Cord Diamondback." A female voice, low and melodious as if it had formal musical training, carried into the saloon from near the entrance. Every man turned to look at the tall woman who hesitantly stood just inside the swinging doors. The men squinted to get a clearer view through the cigar-smoke haze. She stood straight, almost at attention, and wore her loosely bound reddish-brown hair down her back. Her traveling outfit, a brocaded jacket and brown velvet skirt, carried the road's dust but was obviously much too fashionable for a town like Crestview. She waited near the door, head straight out, as if challenging the men's appraisal.

Cord was within a few feet of the door when the woman made her entrance. He walked quickly toward her. "I'm Diamondback," he said. "I've been waiting on this spot for hours." As they walked toward a table he noticed that she seemed to be measuring him.

Cord made his own appraisal. Her features were handsome rather than beautiful. Her chin was too big and her generous mouth was set with determination. The top of her dusty jacket was set with buttons and bows, but couldn't conceal full, rounded breasts. Cord liked her from the moment he saw her challenging the men's leers. She was a woman in a man's place and she wasn't backing down an inch.

"I'm Valerie Blake," the woman said, offering Cord a gloved hand. She looked over his glass-smooth skin that many women found fascinating. "I expected you to be an older man." She glanced up to his rugged face with a puzzled look. "Have we met before, Mr. Diamondback?"

Cord knew he had never met Valerie Blake. He would have remembered. Perhaps she had seen a newspaper sketch of him or a wanted poster.

"Were you in Crestview last Saturday for the big dance?" Cord asked.

"No matter," Valerie said, smiling. "You appear to be competent. I believe my employer will be pleased. He's the person hiring you for this judging assignment. We leave for Denver in an hour to meet him."

"Denver!" Cord laughed. "I rode past Denver on my way to Crestview."

"He wanted this preliminary meeting so I could brief you on your function."

"Fine, only he could have saved my backside three days in the saddle."

Valerie waved her hand, dismissing Cord's backside as of no consequence. "You'll be paid for your trouble. My employer is a powerful man who believes in caution and secrecy."

Cord noticed how formally Valerie spoke, as if she had precise instructions she wished to carry out to the letter. "I thought my function was clear," he said. "I was hired to judge a dispute."

"Of course. However my employer wants me to emphasize that you are to be guided by him." Valerie leaned over and whispered. "Your decision could be very important to this state. As usual, both parties in the dispute believe they are in the right. What is unusual is that they've agreed to arbitration. They've heard about your reputation for fairness and are willing to abide by your decision."

"Which side is your boss on?" Cord asked.

"Neither. His interest is in getting the dispute settled quickly. You're being paid to gather all the facts and present them to my employer. He'll tell you how to make your judgment."

Cord wondered what Valerie and her boss had

heard about his reputation. He smiled, his jaw set firmly. "He's going to tell me what to decide?"

"Yes. He means to be fair. Your reputation won't suffer. I assure you."

"Exactly who is your boss?" Cord asked. His voice had a hard edge to it that made Valerie look up into his dark eyes.

"You'll learn that in Denver."

Cord stood up and tipped his hat. "Thanks for the drink, Miss Blake. Enjoy your trip back to Denver."

"But you're coming with me."

"Afraid not, Miss Blake," Cord said. "My judging services are for sale. Not my decisions. You rode three days for nothing."

Valerie stared at Cord, obviously not believing he was serious. "In that case you're throwing away five thousand dollars and wasted three days, Mr. Diamondback."

Cord grinned thinly. "Not exactly. I'm keeping your five-hundred-dollar advance for the wear and tear on my delicate bottom."

Valerie bit her lip. Her confidence seemed to erode before Cord's determination. "It's extremely important that you return with me, Cord." He noticed the sudden familiar use of his first name. "If I don't complete this assignment, I could be fired."

"The five thousand was a more powerful argument," Cord said.

The foot traffic near Cord's table picked up considerably as men ambled by for a closer inspection of Valerie. She bowed her head closer to

Cord's and whispered seductively. "I can be very appreciative." She laid her gloved hand over Cord's. "Come to Denver with me and I'll show you my gratitude when this is over."

Cord raised an eyebrow. "A fine lady like yourself, sleeping with a scoundrel who accepts a bribe? I couldn't ask you to make that sacrifice. Besides, I've a hunch that's a reward you don't mean for me to collect."

Valerie snatched her hand quickly. "Since money seems to be the only thing that interests you, what if we raise the ante. Will that do it?"

Cord shook his head. There was no point in further conversation. He pushed his chair from the table and rose to leave.

"You'll go!" she threatened, her green eyes narrowing into pinpoints of anger. "Even if I have to force you." She rose quickly from the table, spilling Cord's beer, and ran from the saloon.

Cord was almost sorry. Valerie Blake had spunk and he would have liked to know her better. The chance for five thousand dollars or more had been appealing. But if there were rumors that his decisions were for sale, he'd soon lose all his judging jobs. He wondered where he might go from here. Anyplace, he decided, where no one was likely to recognize him as a wanted assassin. Maybe he could pick up a prizefight in Sacramento.

The bartender came hurrying over. "The lady left without paying. You taking care of her bill?"

"Not me," Cord answered. "Put my drinks on *her* tab."

The bartender's frown showed too much concern over the price of a drink. "I think you better turn around," he whispered, backing slowly away, his eyes white with fear.

Cord spun. He stared into the black, lifeless holes of a double-barreled shotgun.

2

The men standing behind Cord scattered fast, not caring how they slopped their drinks or knocked over their chairs. The fat bartender cursed and snatched as many whiskey bottles from the back of the bar as his chubby fists could hold. The reaction was so fast it seemed practiced. Then Cord noticed the back wall was peppered with buckshot and bullet holes.

"Don't move," Valerie Blake ordered, looking smug and determined, standing near the entrance next to Bearclaws Boone. Bearclaws pointed a 12-gauge blaster straight at Cord's head. That told Cord the mountain man was no expert with the weapon. He was standing too close for an effective shot spread, and a 12-gauge should be aimed at a man's middle so the blast can rip a hole through his guts. His inexperience didn't make Cord feel more comfortable. Bearclaws had the drop on him and there was a crazy glitter in the mountain man's eyes.

"My orders are to bring you back to Denver," Valerie said nervously. "I'm going to show up with your body. The condition it's in is up to you."

How much of it was bluff? Valerie seemed taller than a few minutes ago, but Cord thought he was being influenced by the weapon. A 12-gauge shotgun adds to anyone's height.

"Hey, lady," Bearclaws yelled. "I thought this Injun insulted you. Shit, you want company to Denver, I take you. First I put some holes in him."

"No," Valerie said very quickly. "I'm not looking for a guide." She pointed at Cord. "I need this man for a special job."

"You think he's better than me?" Bearclaws asked walking up to Cord. He punched Diamondback roughly in the chest with the barrel of the shotgun. "This puny fella? I'm a good protector, lady. You got nothing to worry about on the trail when Bearclaws is with you."

"Yes, Miss Blake," Cord said dryly. "Old Bearclaws will keep the wolf away from the campfire. His smell alone is enough to do that."

Bearclaws' face reddened with rage. His fingers twitched on the twin triggers of the shotgun.

Valerie put her hand on the mountain man's arm. "You said you would just use the gun to threaten him," she said desperately. "I don't want him killed. He's no use to me dead." She looked desperately at Cord, her eyes saying she was sorry things had gone so far.

Bearclaws looked lustfully at Valerie as if she were a trapped beaver with a prime pelt. "I show you who is better man now, and I show you who is a better man later tonight."

"You can't prove anything with a shotgun," Cord said.

"That's too much talk for an Injun," Bearclaws said.

Cord laughed. "At least I don't need a shotgun to do my talking."

"Huh?" Bearclaws scowled. "What does that mean?"

"Any puny fellow can pull a trigger. If you're a better man, prove it in a fair fight."

Bearclaws hesitated. His face took on a puzzled look as if he couldn't comprehend what Cord had said. "You want to rassle me?"

"You fight your way and I'll fight mine," Cord said. He pointed at the shotgun. "I'm surprised you feel you need that to handle a puny fellow like me." There was a slight titter in the room.

Bearclaws twisted his head to see who laughed. He raised the 12-gauge skyward. His fingers jerked on the triggers, blasting twin dish-sized holes in the ceiling. Wood splinters drifted to the floor and the patrons saw a hint of blue Colorado sky.

"Damn!" the bartender's voice barked from his hiding place behind the bar. "There goes my rainy-day business."

"I'm goin to put bigger holes in you," Bearclaws taunted. He turned to Valerie. "Tonight you say thanks to me. My way."

The men in the bar broke out in nervous

laughter, their tension released by the shotgun blasts. "Somebody's going to pay for the damage," the bartender said, popping up and showing his gums in an openmouthed grimace.

"Take a cut out of the prize winnings," Cord said.

"What prize winnings?" Bearclaws demanded.

"I don't fight without a stake," Cord said, opening up the space between them in case Bearclaws rushed him. He wondered if he should fight at all. Bearclaws had foolishly discharged the shotgun and Cord still had his Smith and Wesson Schofield .44. The physical threat was gone, so why put himself back in jeopardy? Not because he said he would, the promise was made with a shotgun pointed at his head. But if he refused to fight, the men in the Glory Hole would remember his promise and forget about the shotgun. They'd whisper that Cord Diamondback didn't keep his word.

Bearclaws squinted his eyes at Cord as if trying to get a clearer image. He was obviously accustomed to seeing fear on the faces of the men he attacked. Cord's face was impassive and cool. "You want to bet Bearclaws' money that you'll win?" the mountain man asked.

"Otherwise it's your fists against my Smith and Wesson," Cord declared. "You stopped calling the tune when you fired both barrels of your shotgun." He took out the five-hundred-dollar advance that had lured him to Crestview and waved the money in the air. "This much says I can beat you, mountain man."

Bearclaws backed up a step at the sight of so

many greenbacks. "I got pelts," he finally said. "I'll bet my furs against your money."

Cord shook his head. "Pelts aren't worth anything today," he said. "Put up something of value."

"You're crazy," Valerie said, clutching at Cord's arm to pull him away. "That man looks only half human. He'll probably kill you. Then what will happen to me?"

"The ride to Denver with Bearclaws should be a fascinating experience for you." Cord winked. He was committed now. There was going to be a fight so why not make the stakes as high as possible?

Bearclaws took a beaded pouch with a Shoshone sun design from his pelt. He rummaged through dried fruit, pemmican and beef jerky until he found a smaller felt pouch. "I do some pannin' in the creeks," he said, throwing the small pouch on the bar. "I bet my dust."

Cord hefted the pouch. "There's not five hundred in gold dust here," he said. "Come up with the rest, or find someone who will."

The men in the saloon stared openmouthed at Cord. "You willin' to take on extra bets?" the bartender asked, a crafty look in his eye.

"There's my stake, match it," Cord said.

Will Kincaid turned his jack-o'-lantern grin on Cord. "You look like you done some fighting, mister. But put away your greenbacks. There ain't no such thing as a fair fight against Bearclaws. He'll squash you just for the pure pleasure of hearing your bones break. Why don't you just light out? Save your money and save your hide."

Cord shrugged. "Another day, another dollar."

Men in the bar, realizing the stranger wasn't going to back down, eagerly dug into their pockets, making up the difference between Cord's stake and the dust in Bearclaws' pouch. "Make some elbow room for the contestants," the men demanded when the bets were down.

"Not here," the bartender shouted. "You gents ain't wrecking my establishment. These glasses come from St. Louis. Bust 'em, and you'll be drinking whiskey out of your boots."

"Couldn't tell the difference with the swill you serve," an old man with a red, bulbous nose observed.

"Take the fight out to the street," the bartender said.

"No good," Kincaid said. "There's decent women in this town. We can't have brawling and bloodletting in the streets. There's some females as is too delicate for those sights."

"Why not Boot Hill?" the bartender asked.

"Isn't there any law in this town?" Valerie asked, looking around frantically. "Can't someone stop this?"

"Boot Hill," the bartender said again, pushing his suggestion. "It's close enough so the walk ain't going to tire anybody. And there's enough room up there for both of them to thresh about all they please."

"Anywhere," Bearclaws yelled. "I'm tired of all this palaver."

Will Kincaid grabbed Cord's sleeve. "Last chance to skedaddle," he said.

"Too late now," Cord said.

"Never too late to save your own skin," Kincaid replied. "I've seen Bearclaws fight three men in as many years. One of 'em has an oak leg that was just fine before old Bearclaws started gnawing and yanking on it."

Cord swallowed dryly, wincing. "And the other two men he fought?"

"We're going to visit them right now," Kincaid said. "On Boot Hill."

3

"Men are such infants," Tessie Krebs said as she bustled up Boot Hill, skirts raised delicately to keep them out of the dust. "They fight over everything."

"That's one reason I never married," replied Amanda Applegate, the town's lone spinster, who followed hard on Tessie's heels. In this part of Colorado, men outnumbered women fve to one, so any unmarried lady over twenty-five felt the need for a large warehouse of excuses.

Boot Hill wasn't really a hill, just a small rise outside the west end of town. Most of the graves had wooden markers, the lettering fading fast as the wood weathered. A few sites were piled with stones, keeping out the varmints and weighing down the dead. A freshly dug grave, for one Sam Parsons, who had been kicked in the head by his horse and was due to be buried tomorrow, was in

one corner of the cemetery. The marker, lettered,
"Sam Parsons, kicked by a mare, life ain't fair,"
had been composed by Adelaide Parsons, Sam's
wife and the only person in town with literary
pretentions. It was her first published work. Sam's
marker lay next to his grave awaiting his arrival.

"Looks like we're a grave short," Tessie Krebs
shouted as she approached the impromptu arena.
Tessie was one of the womenfolk considered to be
too refined to watch a bloody fistfight.

The crowd formed a ring near the fresh gravesite.
A few men hoisted young children on their shoulders for better views of the proceedings. Bearclaws
and Cord stood inside the ring separated by Will
Kincaid, chosen as referee because as town barber
he shaved the throats of every man in town and
had to be trusted.

Bearclaws pulled his filthy buckskin shirt from
his huge torso.

"I reckon that thing ain't been washed since the
blizzard of '72," Amanda Applegate observed. "Him
neither."

The mountain man's muscles rounded out against
his hairy arms like cannonballs. He had no neck.
His head rested directly on his shoulders like a
pumpkin sitting on a shelf. At the end of his
unnaturally long arms, furry paws dangled with fat
fingers that looked like miniature black snakes.
The fingers were tipped with thick jagged nails
untrimmed for thirty years. The nails looked like
talons. Crusted with dirt, they curved downward
into dangerous points that could slash a man's skin,

rip through muscle, cut straight through to the bone.

Bearclaws' naked chest was covered with partially healed scratches and even a few toothmarks, representing the futile and desperate efforts of unsuccessful opponents from dozens of rough-and-tumble fights. The crowd buzzed.

Cord almost smiled. What would the crowd say if his own scarred back was revealed? What if they saw the white scar tissue ridged like the pattern of a Diamondback rattler? Unlike the snake, Cord couldn't shed his skin for a fresh covering. The brand was permanent, marking him now and forever as a fugitive and killer.

The sight of Bearclaws' forbidding presence set the crowd shivering. A few of the more refined women, including the spinster, Amanda Applegate, pretended to block their eyes with loosely held fingers that permitted full vision.

"He's mated to a she-panther," Tessie Krebs whispered.

The whisper, delivered with a hiss that carried through the crowd, set them thinking about the possibility. The people continued to swap old stories about Bearclaws, half believing them, adding new lies and half believing them too.

Cord ignored the whispers. He wouldn't allow his own intensity to be broken as he focused on the fight ahead. He dammed away all other thoughts, sending extra strength and determination surging into his taut muscles. As iron is made into steel by the addition of trace elements, Cord had been hardened and tempered by life as a

fugitive. Any softness had melted away. He felt
his juices bubbling. A mixture of excitement and
fear rose in his mouth, tasting sharp and sweet,
like a heavy rum. He whipped himself into a
battle frenzy like the Scandinavian Berserker of
Viking days. He was ready!

"Take off your shirt, Diamondback!" Kincaid
called to Cord.

Cord's lips formed a tight smile without mirth.
"I may not work up a sweat."

"Suit yourself," Bearclaws snarled. "You're just
giving me something else to grab hold of."

Valerie tugged at Cord's arm in a last-ditch
effort to haul him away. "This isn't what I wanted,"
she said. "You don't have to prove yourself."

Cord put his arms around her shoulders and
guided her to the other spectators. "Enjoy the
fight," he told her. "You started it."

"There ain't no rules," Kincaid said as he raised
his arms to quiet the crowd. "After this fracas
starts, my services will be limited to declaring a
winner. Come at each other until one man says
he'd had enough, or can't say nothing." Kincaid
raised his hand, held it poised to show he had
control and dramatically swept the hand to his
side. "Go!"

Bearclaws rushed straight across the space sepa-
rating him from Cord Diamondback as if his body
had been on a railroad track. Cord stood his ground
coolly, anxious now for the first contact, the first
test of strength and will. The mountain man let
out a terrible sound that was half roar, half growl
as he closed the ground between them. Cord side-

stepped the ponderous charge easily, throwing a quick right hook into the mountain man's bread-basket. The blow ricocheted off his rock-hard stomach like a drop of rain off a pane of glass—and did as little damage. As Bearclaws hurtled by, Cord dug a hard elbow into his spinal column. Bearclaws skidded into the grass, his knees crushing the daiseys on the well-tended grave of Silas Toomey.

The mountain man rose slowly, shaking his head. He advanced toward Cord, more carefully this time, arms outstretched like a lover seeking to embrace a reluctant sweetheart. Cord backpedaled, shifting direction with quick feints, always keeping a good angle of attack. Bearclaws followed the direction changes impatiently. He took several long, open-handed swipes at Cord, nails outstretched like miniature daggers. Each swipe missed Cord by at least a foot.

He obviously relies on brute strength, Cord thought. The way he comes at me, not bothering to protect himself, means he's prepared to take five blows to give one.

"Stand still, dammit," Bearclaws roared as Cord continued to stay out of reach.

Cord punctuated the "dammit" with a left jab and straight right to the mountain man's mouth. Blood spurted from his lips like a tiny geyser and spotted his gray-streaked beard. Cord stayed on his toes, weaving and peppering Bearclaws with short, sharp punches to the head and body. He moved in and out of range so quickly Bearclaws had no time to retaliate.

Bearclaws waved wildly at Cord's punches as if

he were trying to catch a stinging bee. He plod-
ded forward like a man on his way to work.

"That Diamondback is giving old Bearclaws some
trouble," Amanda Applegate observed.

"Naw, them's love pats," Tessie Krebs replied.
"What Diamondback is doin' now will make it
worse for him once Bearclaws gets him in his bear
hug."

Valerie flitted on the edges of the human ring
that expanded or contracted as the fighters moved.
She seemed to be looking for allies in stopping the
fight.

The dimensions of the arena kept shifting so
Cord never knew how far he could backpedal
before needing to change directions. He backed
into a chubby woman who was lifting her skirts to
scuttle away, and barely avoided Bearclaws' lunge.
The mountain man fell into the crowd, dragging
the woman and a teenage boy to the ground with
him.

Cord skipped and bobbed, moving in to sting
Bearclaws and then stepping away, matching his
opponent's strength with his skill, the mountain
man's weight with his guile.

The crowd shifted too lazily behind the retreating Cord. He spun to change direction and tripped
over the bartender's outstretched foot.

"Foul," shouted Valerie, "he bet against Diamondback."

Bearclaws loped in fast, reaching Cord as he
was rising. The mountain man swiped with one of
his huge paws, nails extended like razors, toward
Cord's chest. Cord jumped back fast to avoid the

blow, but the sharp points slashed through the skin of his forearm, gouging out long chunks of flesh. Blood gushed from his arm wounds, soaking his shirt and trousers a crimson red. The piercing pain reminded Cord of the time he'd been accidentally gaffed with a whaling harpoon.

"First serious blood," Kincaid announced.

"Yep," the bartender replied, obviously feeling better about his wager. "This Diamondback can dance all he wants, but sooner or later Bearclaws is going to catch up with him."

Cord retreated, trying to keep one eye on Bearclaws, the other on the moving crowd at his back. His left arm hung uselessly at his side. Bearclaws swooped in faster than Cord thought possible, swinging his unnaturally long arm like a scythe. The nails raked Cord across the chest. His skin piled up like accordian folds at the ends of long divits across his pectoral muscles. Some tissue stuck to the end of Bearclaws' dirty fingernails, like paper from a torn package. Blood poured from the wounds, drenching Cord's already stained shirt, flowing down his stomach and seeping into old graves.

Cord felt his strength escaping with the blood that flowed from his body. His muscles felt tired as if he'd been awake and on his feet for two days. His quickness was gone.

Bearclaws moved relentlessly toward Cord, windmilling his arms to take advantage of his long reach. The crowd inched in closer, tightening the ring. Cord needed an opening. He knew he had to do something outrageous that would enrage

Bearclaws, make him lose control. As Bearclaws repeated one of his endless charges Cord stood stock still, like a suicide hypnotized by the light of an onrushing train. The crowd gasped. Bearclaws' arms extended toward Cord, offering a fatal sanctuary. Cord dropped to his back, kicked his feet into Bearclaws' stomach and lifted. The mountain man rose from the ground, suspended on Cord's feet. Cord flexed his knees and kicked out with all his strength. Bearclaws' body went flying, landing on a nearby rockpile that marked a grave.

The mountain man rose quickly. He turned to face Cord, his body shaking with rage.

The crowd yipped with delight. "Did you see that? He kicked old Bearclaws into the sky."

The tiny glitter of insanity Cord had seen in Bearclaws' eyes burned with a greater intensity. He charged across the graveyard, completely out of control. His arms flailed like pistons on a steam engine.

Good, Cord thought. If he stays out of control long enough, I can win. But it must be soon.

Cord could feel the strength ebbing out of him. He sidestepped Bearclaws' charge and clubbed the mountain man across the side of his head with a right fist. Cord felt he'd smashed his hand into an adobe wall. Bearclaws came back again like he was a ferryboat coming and going across the same river. Cord ducked under the mountain man's outstretched arms, reached his good hand below Bearclaws' knees and flipped him on his head.

Bearclaws landed on his skull, groaned once and lay still. Cord moved in to finish him off. He could hear the mountain man's desperate breathing. Cord's blood continued to ebb from his wounds, sapping the little strength he had left. Bearclaws struggled to one knee. Cord smashed him across the back of his neck with a savage rabbit punch. Bearclaws groaned like an animal caught in barbed wire. His body flattened to the ground.

"I think the stranger's done it," Tessie Krebs commented.

"Let's wait a minute," Kincaid cautioned. "There's plenty of money riding on this."

Cord advanced cautiously, looking for signs that Bearclaws might be playing possum. The mountain man's breathing seemed suspiciously strong for a man who was supposed to be unconscious. Cord saw an eyelid flicker. Boone was faking! The trick seemed amateurish. Cord brought his foot back for the kick to the head that would finish Bearclaws once and for all. Suddenly the mountain man twisted his body and snaked an arm around Cord's leg. Bearclaws clutched an ankle in his huge paw and pulled Cord to the ground.

Cord cursed himself. He'd hesitated in striking an apparently unconscious man, his eastern sensibilities still stubbornly hanging on. But this wasn't polite society, it wasn't the Harvard Yard. This was the West and his moment of weakness would cost him.

Bearclaws rose to his feet, picking Cord up as effortlessly as if he was a sack of flour. His ugly face contorted with effort as he encircled Cord in his Neanderthal-like arms and squeezed. His cannonball muscles stood out hard and round, glisten-

ing with sweat, the veins popping out in blue
relief from his strain.

Cord felt the breath being pressed out of him
like a slowly closing bellows. The blood flowing
from his chest wounds covered Bearclaws' hairy
body. Cord could smell the stench of the mountain man's rancid bear grease, reminding him of
the days when his whaling ship boiled blubber.

"The stranger's done," someone commented.
"If no griz ever broke that hold, how can he? Hey,
Kincaid. Get old Bearclaws to ease off. We won
our money. No use killing this stranger."

"I'm giving Diamondback the same chance I
gave Bearclaws." Kincaid said. "I got no money
down, so I ain't as anxious as you to see this
settled."

Cord couldn't take in air. The oxygen already in
his system would keep him alive another minute
or two. Only the excruciating pain as his chest
buckled under Bearclaws' pressure kept him from
going under. A red film, gradually turning black,
blotted out all other sight. Cord Diamondback
only had a few more seconds of life.

Cord's arms were pinioned. He could feel his
ribs crushed to the breaking point. Bearclaws had
the upper half of Cord's body bent backward so he
had no leverage for a kick to the balls. Cord
pulled his head forward, moving close to Bearclaws'
face as if he intended to give the mountain man a
kiss. Cord opened his mouth wide and snapped
his teeth down hard on Bearclaws' nose. He felt
his teeth crunching through cartilage and bone.
His mouth tasted salty from Bearclaws' blood. As

he pulled his head away he heard the soft tear of flesh as his teeth still clenched on the mountain man's nostrils. He spit out chunks of skin and bits of cartilage as the mountain man's thick blood dribbled down his chin.

Bearclaws screamed in agony. He dropped Cord, moving his hands up to his face.

Cord noted, with satisfaction, the deep indentations across Bearclaws' nose. He smashed his forehead into the open wound and felt more bone give way. Cord belted Bearclaws with punches to his unguarded midsection. The mountain man fell ponderously, like a redwood tree that had been chopped off at the base. He grunted low and guttural and rose quickly. Cord wondered if he could ever put him down permanently. The man seemed capable of absorbing an unlimited amount of pain. He kept coming on!

Cord was bone weary. He wished he had the luxury of a second to recover. He retreated, hoping the crowd behind him would melt as the fight moved their way. He had a vague notion he was backing toward Sam Parsons' open gravesite, but he didn't dare turn his head away from Bearclaws to make certain.

Bearclaws stormed toward Cord, apparently as fresh as when he made his first charge. Cord feinted too slowly, his muscles failing to respond now. The mountain man smacked him a solid shot to the head that knocked him backward into a hole. He felt himself tumble through space, finally landing on his head and shoulder. Pain jolted through his body as his spine made cracking noises. Sam Parsons' grave had a tenant a day early.

Cord lay at the bottom of the pit, dazed. The freshly dug earth felt cool and restful. He slowly struggled to his feet, digging his fingers into the crumbly earthen side walls. The top of Cord's head came flush to the top of the pit. He didn't belong in the bottom of a grave, but resurrection appeared difficult, especially with Bearclaws hovering topside.

Cord reached his right hand and elbow up top. He strained to pull himself out, but his head reeled as Bearclaws bashed him alongside the ear with a wooden board. The blow sent Cord slipping back down into the floor of the grave, loosening dirt on top of him.

"Don't you go breaking Sam's marker," Cord heard a female voice shout. He realized Bearclaws had hit him with Parsons' grave marker.

Cord shook his head to clear it. He dug a foothold into one of the grave walls and tried boosting himself up. The wall collapsed. As Cord fell to the floor more dirt cascaded over his body. Cord moved to the other side. He bobbed his head topside and barely avoided being crowned by another vicious swing of the marker. He couldn't locate Bearclaws, but if he didn't get out soon, he knew he'd faint from loss of blood.

"This is like a shooting gallery," Amanda Applegate shouted.

If I can't go up, I'll go down, Cord thought. He huddled in the bottom of the grave and stayed there.

Silence up top.

"Is it over?" Cord heard Kincaid ask after a while. "Diamondback, have you had enough?"

Cord hunkered further down into his pit.

"He's probably dead," Cord heard the bartender say. "Let's kick dirt on him and go home."

"You claimin' victory, Bearclaws?" Kincaid asked.

Cord smelled rancid bear grease. He saw a forehead, then the insane glitter in Bearclaws' eyes. A dirty gray, bloodstained beard dangled down the side of the grave like a fishline in a quiet pool. Cord leaped up and yanked on the beard with both hands. Bearclaws' mouth was finally revealed as he screamed. It was a mean little mouth housing a few blackened teeth and a great many tooth stumps. The mountain man tumbled into the grave, landing right on top of Cord Diamondback.

Cord couldn't move as the weight of Bearclaws' huge body pinned him to the earth floor. The mountain man was stunned by his fall, but Cord could feel him stirring. He had to get free!

Cord pulled his right hand loose. Bearclaws blinked his red eyes, fully conscious now. He half turned and stretched his talonlike nails toward Cord's face.

"I'm going to slash your eyes out," Bearclaws snarled, razing his nails across Cord's cheek.

Cord clenched his hand into a fist. He struck upward with all his might, using the fist like a pilehammer. The blow smashed directly into Bearclaws' Adam's apple, forcing it into the mountain man's windpipe. Cord felt like he had cracked a walnut with his bare fist.

Bearclaws gasped. He clutched his throat as if
he could torture it into breathing air. His face
turned red as his blood-soaked beard. Rattling
sounds came from his throat as spittle formed
around the corners of his mouth. His body flopped
spasmodically, giving Cord a chance to slip out
from under the mountain man's frame.

Faces peered down from the top of the grave.

"Man who comes up first is the winner, I reckon,"
said Kincaid.

"Appears they're both dead. Supposin' nobody
comes up?"

"Then I guess we got us a draw."

Cord tried willing his body out of the grave.

He dug a foothold in the side of the grave, but
the crumbling earth wouldn't support his weight.
All his strength was gone, used up in that last
blow. He rose slowly only to slip again, landing
heavily on Bearclaws' body. The mountain man
moaned softly, his face turning a delicate shade of
purple. Cord forced his body up for one last effort.

The highest point in the grave was Bearclaws'
head. Cord tilted the head carefully to the left,
but it slumped over to Bearclaws' shoulder. Cord
adjusted the head again, pushing it back so it
rested against the side of the grave. He placed
one foot on Bearclaws' chest and the other on his
face. The mountain man's body provided the
stepping-stone he needed. Cord managed a hand
and then an elbow topside. He had never worked
so hard in toeing the mark. He pushed one leg
over. The crowd cheered him wildly, even a few
who'd bet against him.

Cord felt a hand slip around his other ankle in a viselike grip. He clutched a clump of grass to keep from falling back in the grave as the hand tugged at him, the talonlike nails puncturing his flesh. Cord looked down at Bearclaws. The mountain man's huge paw fell away and flopped across his chest. He was done. The hand had been a reflex action, like a chicken running around a barnyard for several minutes after its head has been cut off.

Cord staggered to his feet. The crowd gathered round, a few sour faces showing they'd bet a different man would emerge from the pit.

"Is he dead?" Kincaid asked as they tried to hoist the mountain man out of Sam Parsons' reserved space.

Cord shrugged. "If you have a doctor in town who knows how to slit a man's throat to let air in, I think he'll live."

"I can do that," Kincaid said indignantly. "I'm the town barber."

"I'll take my winnings now," Cord said. He felt his head reel as Sam's face lost focus.

"I'll hold the money for him," Cord heard Valerie say. He had forgotten about her. He had forgotten about everything. His knees felt as crumbly as the grave's earthen walls as he toppled backward into the open pit.

4

Cord rested easily in a cool mountain stream created by melting snow from the peaks above. The icy waters refreshed his aching body, but the stream teemed with big rainbow trout with sharp teeth. As the trout swam by they snapped at Cord's body, painfully tearing away small pieces of his flesh. A five-pounder wriggled near and ripped away a good-size chunk of his arm.

He awoke swearing.

Valerie Blake stood over him holding a bottle of French champagne. She spilled a small puddle of the wine on his bare chest and gently massaged it into his skin. The bubbly liquid seeping into the wounds made by Bearclaws' slashing nails created a sharp stinging sensation that made Cord realize he wasn't dreaming this time.

Valerie smiled when she saw him wince. "I'm giving you an alcohol rub to wash out your wounds," she said. "The bartender had a bottle of champagne left over from the time that Lily Langtry passed through town. It was the only thing he had that wouldn't do more harm than good."

Cord watched her pour more champagne onto his chest and move her slim hands over his stomach and arms. He wondered if that were real concern he saw in her green eyes. Her hands lingered over his lean, tempered muscles. Where his skin was unmarked, the effervescent wine hissed and foamed, soothing and cooling his body. Where he had been cut or the skin was broken, the liquid seared and burned like a flash of open gunpowder.

The room was lit by a single kerosene lamp with the wick set low. The lamp cast a golden glow, backlighting Valerie's reddish-brown hair.

"I always thought that champagne had more medicinal value when taken internally," Cord said. He tried to sit up but collapsed back on the bed.

Valerie put the bottle to his lips and let him take several long gulps before snatching it away. She moved her hands lower on Cord's body, massaging the champagne into his hips and inner thighs. He realized he was stark naked. Valerie didn't seem to mind. Her cool hands moved upward, stirring him despite his pain. She saw the reaction and glanced up into his face with a tiny smile.

She must have seen the scars on his back! Then she knew that he wasn't Cord Diamondback, but Christopher Deacon, the alleged murderer of Senator Fallows. Everyone knew the story, or thought they did. Cord had killed Fallows, that much was true. But the senator wasn't a man, he was a predatory monster who controlled prostitution, gambling, opium and every other slimy racket on the Barbary Coast. Cord's brother had found out about Fallows and was killed for knowing. What Cord did to the senator wasn't murder, it was retribution.

Cord couldn't expect Valerie to understand. Not after the newspapers had written about him as the vilest assassin since John Wilkes Booth. He scanned the room for his Smith and Wesson Schofield .44. The gun was nowhere in sight.

She must have sensed his panic. "Yes, I've seen the scars. I know who you are."

"And?" Cord asked.

"Will Kincaid was ignoring your wounds to work on Bearclaws' throat," Valerie said, ignoring Cord's question. "You looked in bad shape, so I had two men bring you up to my room. I stripped your clothes and managed to stop the bleeding. Some of Bearclaws' gouges went bone deep and his nails were filthy. I got quite a surprise when I turned you over and saw your back."

"You did all this so I'd return with you?"

Her mouth turned down in disappointment. "Of course," she said sarcastically. "I couldn't have helped because I cared what happened to you." She smiled slightly, half to herself. "I didn't know murderers had as many scruples as you pretend to have."

"Don't you know what happened?" Cord asked grimly.

"Yes, the newspapers were very specific. Grisly even."

"They didn't tell the whole story," Cord said.

"I'm sure you were justified," Valerie said, looking as if she didn't believe it. "But I'm not concerned about your past. Actually your problem solves my problem. Call it blackmail if you will, but you'd better be in shape to travel tomorrow."

Cord sat up in bed, ignoring his nakedness. "Actually what you're attempting is extortion, not blackmail." His rugged face looked dangerous.

"What's the difference?"

"Blackmail involves a written threat."

"Who cares about legal definitions?" Valerie cried.

"Just part of my professional service. I feel you should have something for your five hundred dollars."

"I will have something," she threatened. "I'll have you in Denver."

"And if I refuse, you'll tell everyone I'm Christopher Deacon?"

"In a second," she said. Then almost sobbing, she added, "I don't know what else to do."

Cord could see the tears welling up in her green eyes. Earlier he would have doubted their sincerity. Now he wasn't so sure. Still, he wasn't about to make the same mistake with her he'd made with Bearclaws.

"You don't know what my employer will do if I don't succeed. What other solution is there?"

"Just tell him I can't be bribed to make a decision."

Valerie's face brightened. "Why don't you tell him yourself? Then he can't say I didn't do my job." She dabbed at her face with a handkerchief.

"I think you owe me something. You might have died if I hadn't nursed your wounds."

"If it wasn't for you, I wouldn't have been forced into a fight in the first place," Cord said.

"Not my fault," Valerie replied. "You could have shot Bearclaws after he emptied his shotgun into the ceiling."

"That's not the way things are done out here," Cord said. "Not if you want to work again as a judge. Which reminds me, you definitely owe me something. Where are my prize winnings?"

Valerie reached for her purse and scattered greenbacks over Cord's legs and torso. "There's your money," she said. "Spend it in Denver."

"I'm convinced," Cord said. "Your boss is desperate to see me."

Valerie brightened. "Then you'll go?"

Cord frowned as if he was trying to work something out. "I'll have to tell him that you almost got me killed. I wonder if he had any use for a dead judge?"

She gasped. "But I never meant for—"

"Results are what count," Cord said. "I'm sure he'll be interested in how you handled the situation."

She looked at him angrily. "You would tell him, wouldn't you? You're trying to blackmail me."

"It's still extortion," Cord reminded her. "And yes I would. Why don't we call this match a draw? If I don't come to Denver, I can't tell your boss what you did."

Valerie seemed thoroughly deflated, as if her

last hope was gone. "A draw means I lose," she said. "All right. I'll say I couldn't find you."

Now that the threat was removed, Cord felt himself intrigued by the job. If only he knew more. He felt pleased that Cord Diamondback's reputation had grown enough that two factions were willing to accept his decision. And the promised five thousand was enticing. That sum, plus what he had won today, would keep him for a long time. He thought about explaining to Valerie's boss that his value as a judge depended on his impartiality. The chance for a season without money worries was worth the ride to Denver. There was another reason. Could he trust Valerie to keep quiet about the scars on his back? He saw how she caved in under pressure. What would she say when her boss grilled her?

"What if I agree to go with you after all?" Cord asked.

"Do you mean it?"

Cord nodded.

Valerie ran to him and threw both arms around his neck. The buttons on her eastern dress dug into the gouges on his body, causing him to push her away. "That hurts!"

She moved back, offended. "I was just trying to show my gratitude."

"A handshake will be sufficient," Cord said.

She advanced again and playfully stuck out her hand. When Cord put his own hand forward, she pulled him to her and kissed him on the lips. Her other hand rested on his thigh near his penis. She glanced down and smiled as his penis lengthened.

Valerie broke off her kiss and began unbuttoning her dress.

"That's not necessary," Cord said quietly. "Your body isn't part of the bargain."

She looked up quickly. "I want to, Cord. I've wanted to since I first undressed you."

Valerie undressed quickly, glancing frequently at Cord to see if he was paying attention. She hesitated for a moment when she was down to her underwear, but that fell to the floor with her dress and petticoats. She stood at the foot of the bed, her body backlit by a golden halo cast by the kerosene lamp. Her breasts were large and firm with dark brown nipples, already hardening.

Valerie was a natural redhead all right. Her pubic patch was a flame of red hair smoldering away at her vagina. She moved closer toward where Cord lay on the bed. He forgot the pain of his wounds as his penis stiffened.

Valerie stood over him, her vagina less than a foot from his mouth. He bent his head forward and tenderly kissed her vagina, like a lover kissing his sweetheart on the lips. She sighed and put one knee on the bed, moving her body still closer to his face. She had rubbed perfume onto her genitals, but Cord could smell her sex underlying the flowery scent. The odor was similar to strong Chinese tea.

Cord stroked his finger along the length of her vagina, penetrating just below the surface like a miner working a shallow claim. She bent her body forward and grasped his penis in her long fingers. They felt cool and sticky from the champagne and

Cord's skin rode along as she pumped her hand up and down. His penis grew purply red as blood rushed into the area, packing it thick and hard.

Cord replaced his finger with his tongue. Her gasp of pleasure encouraged him to push the tongue deep inside her vagina, her musky essence saturating his taste buds.

"So sweet," she said. Valerie climbed onto the bed, straddling his face with her knees, and bent over his penis. She took it in both hands, holding it close to her eyes for inspection. "So sweet," she said again as she placed the tip into her mouth. Her hand stroked his shaft as her tongue flicked again and again at the crack in his tip. Cord felt ready to boil over, but each time he came close, she'd nip his penis hard, forcing his juices back down.

Her right hand moved down to his testicles, squeezing not too gently. She swallowed more and more of Cord's shaft into her mouth and down her throat until her lips were kissing the hand holding his testicles. Cord felt imprisoned in a warm, wet, wonderful sea. Her head bobbed up and down on his shaft in a milking action. Cord bucked his hips up into her face.

"Not yet," she said, taking his penis out of her mouth and holding it against her cheek.

She settled down comfortably on his face. Cord put his hands on the cheeks of her round ass, guiding her vagina toward his mouth. He moved his head forward, stroking the length of her vagina with his tongue. Her breath hissed.

"Do that again," she asked.

Valerie pushed her hips down, rubbing her genitals across Cord's face harder and harder. She bent over again, swallowing his penis, her mouth working wildly, moving her lips and tongue. She used her hands to squeeze his testicles like she was trying to squeeze liquid out of a syringe.

Cord's skin glistened with her juices as she rubbed her sex into his face. She clamped her thighs across the cheeks of his face, imprisoning him in soft, feminine flesh. She braced, her body coming to attention, and let out a muffled scream. Her clitoris danced across Cord's tongue like grease on a hot griddle. Her thighs quivered out of control against Cord's cheeks.

Cord felt his penis was in a whirlpool, being sucked deeper and deeper. He raised his hips, pushing hard into her face until he spurted into her mouth and down her throat. Valerie worked his balls, her sucking sounds noisy as she drew in air along with Cord's juices. Cord's penis throbbed in her mouth as his semen drained out of him.

Valerie's finger traced the Diamondback pattern on Cord's back. "Not many men out west are willing to make love the French way," she said as they lay side by side, exhausted. Her hands kept sliding over his rock-hard muscles as if she couldn't quite believe what she was feeling. "They'll take it of course, but so few westerners are prepared for *soixante-neuf*. You're a damned funny cowboy, Cord Diamondback, or Christopher Deacon, or whatever your name really is. Where did you learn how to please a woman?"

"I read a lot," Cord said.

She laughed. "The advantages of being a book-worm."

Her hand was on his penis again. She was kneading it, like dough, and like dough, his penis was rising. She kissed him on the lips, opening her mouth and drawing in his tongue. Cord could taste himself as their tongues dueled.

Cord slid his hand between Valerie's legs, moving the palm across her vagina, still wet and sweaty from their previous lovemaking.

She sighed, rolling on her back and spreading her legs. Her flame-red pubic hair made it seem as if he were plunging his penis into the mouth of an erupting volcano. He pushed his penis past the mouth of the volcano into the hot lava below. Valerie moved up her knees to make a saddle for Cord between her thighs. She tightened her vaginal muscles around his shaft. He moved inside her slowly, wanting to make it last. One of her hands petted his ass while the other gently played with his testicles.

Each time Cord stroked downward she moved her body up to meet him. He increased the tempo, pounding into her faster. Their bodies thudded together, making wet, slapping noises. Small grunts came from her throat. Her face contorted as if the pleasure was unbearable. Cord felt he was penetrating her to the core. Her pelvis jumped off the bed to meet his descending penis more than halfway. Her body seemed so out of control Cord didn't think they could stay on the bed. Her nipples against his chest seemed hard as small walnuts. Her legs wrapped around his back. Cord slid both hands to her ass cheeks, pulling himself deeper inside her.

"More," she said, throwing her head back. Cord pumped harder, feeling his semen rushing toward the tip of his shaft. Her vagina twitched and spasmed as he shot into her. She grabbed his face with both hands and gave him an openmouthed kiss while her volcano kept erupting. Her tongue caromed around the corners of his mouth like an overplayed three-cushion billiard shot. Cord heard whimpering sounds from her throat as her orgasm seemed to go on forever.

Valerie curled herself around the contour of Cord's body as if she were fused to him. "I'm going to remember the trip to Denver for a long, long time," she said. "We're taking the stage, so we'll have an extra day together."

"I'll enjoy the time with you," he said. "But I thought you were in a hurry to get back."

"I'll feel safer riding in company."

Cord didn't understand her strange remark, but he was exhausted in a sexual afterglow. He'd ask her about it in the morning. Almost dozing, he gently stroked her body as she nuzzled into him. He wrapped his arm around her back, and she broke away from him with a small cry of pain.

"What's the matter?"

"Nothing."

Cord got out of bed and turned up the kerosene lamp. "Let me see your back."

Valerie reluctantly turned on her side. Welts and bruises covered her back from shoulder blades to waist. The welts were long and narrow, as if they'd been raised by something like a riding crop. The bruises were everywhere, old and discolored to a blackish purple. One small bruise pattern, three points in the form of a triangle, seemed to be repeated several times.

"Who did this?" Cord asked.

"Don't ask me to explain, it's too humiliating." She wore her fright like a ragged winter coat.

Cord didn't have to ask again. The bruises on Valerie's back must be the work of her employer. That was the reason for her terror. Suddenly he was anxious to meet Valerie's boss.

5

"At least it's a Concord," Cord sighed as he tied his Morgan behind the bright red stage. The New England–made coach had the reputation of providing a smooth ride because the body was strung on ox-hide straps in lieu of springs. Cord noticed the driver was hitching up a spike team of five mules, which meant they were in for a rough road.

Valerie packed her luggage in the leather boot at the rear. Cord threw his Springfield up top where the driver put it under his seat alongside the water bucket and buffalo robes.

The driver was a grizzled man in his fifties with an overgrown mustache turning white at the bottom so it appeared like it was disappearing into his mouth. Years of high-country sun had burned and thickened his skin until it looked blacker and tougher than the leather curtains covering the open coach windows.

"How far you takin' Holladay's Overland?" the driver asked Cord. Ben Holladay had sold the stage line to Wells Fargo years ago, but some veteran drivers still used the old name.

"Denver," Cord said, shading his eyes as he squinted at the driver.

The driver put a pinch of snuff into his nostril and waited until it settled. "Company ain't making money this trip," he said. "We got two other passengers and a messenger riding up top with me."

Cord knew they were hauling something valuable or they expected trouble. "Messenger" was just a fancy name for guard.

The inside of the coach seated nine, with room on the arching roof for six more. Because there were so few passengers, Cord asked the driver to remove the leather seat in the middle.

Their fellow passengers stepped into the coach and nodded politely. They were dressed like farmers, a couple grown prematurely old from long years in the fields.

Cord felt the coach shift down under the weight of the driver and the messenger. The driver cracked his whip over the heads of the mules and they were on their way.

The team started slowly, but the coach still swayed with a lateral motion that reminded Cord of sailing through a choppy ocean during his whaling days. As speed increased, the spoked wooden wheels mercilessly found every rut and stone in the rough dirt road. The coach pitched and dipped, jostling their bodies and crunching their bones. As he and Valerie bounced on the wooden seats Cord felt he had weathered hurricanes no worse than this.

The hot afternoon sun turned the inside of the coach into an oven. Valerie wiped the perspiration from her forehead, a fixed smile on her lips. Dust and sand blew through the curtains' openings and plastered to the passengers' sweaty faces, making them look like ghosts.

"Ain't a rocking chair, hey?" the farmer said to Cord. He extended a gnarled hand across the coach. "Folks journeying should howdy. I'm Ham Smolley. This is my wife Beulah."

Cord introduced himself and Valerie. "Where you headed?" he asked.

"Gilpin County," Ham said. "I hear there's still some color to be dug out of Gregory Gulch." Ham's face had the texture of corrugated iron that had been left to rust.

"You don't have the look of a prospector," Cord said.

Ham laughed without humor. "I been diggin' in the dirt for more than forty-five years," he said. "Never paid me back nothing anyways."

His wife laid her hand on top of his. "That's not true, Ham. We did fine in Pennsylvania before the war."

Ham nodded wistfully. "Wish we was back there. Got through the war without losing a single crop. Our place was less than twenty miles from Gettysburg. Armies from both sides passed near my farm plenty of times. I thought we was charmed. Then, after the war, my own neighbors forced us off the place." He paused, trying to determine their sympathies, forgetting he was speaking to the next generation. "We was Butternuts," he finally admitted proudly.

"What's that?" Valerie asked.

"They were northern farmers who supported peace during the Civil War," Cord told her. "It's a reference to their home-dyed clothes."

"Copperheads," Ham said. "That's what they called us. So we come out here. First year, our daughter died of mountain sickness. I had it myself, but Beulah pulled me through by boiling sagebrush down to a thick syrup and feeding it to me five times a day. Didn't work for our little girl. Nothing's gone right since."

Ham Smolley fell silent as the stage headed north, roughly following the track of the Goodnight-Loving cattle trail. At some point the driver obviously planned to turn west or the road would have taken them to Cheyenne.

After twenty-five miles of bone bruising, the driver mercifully stopped at a swing station. The station house had been built with stone walls to withstand Indian attacks. Outside, a stable and corral housed spare horse and mule teams. The house itelf had two small rooms sparsely furnished with one table, a few cots and half a dozen three-legged stools. Like many station houses, the fireplace concealed the entrance to a tunnel providing an escape route in case an Indian raid got too hot.

"This place has never seen a broom," Beulah Smolley said as the passengers walked in.

The driver unhitched the mule team and came

into the station house with the messenger. Cord caught his first glimpse of him. He was a tall young man, thin as a cadaver and no more talkative. He must have been impressed by the Hickok stories, because the butt end of two army Colts and a Bowie knife protruded from a broad sash he wore around his waist.

"May as well have names all around," the driver said as they dug into the venison stew provided by the station master. "I'm Billy Grimes, been driving this line since '70. This well-heeled, talkative, desperado next to me is Dick Beamer. First jaunt with the company, ain't it, Dickie?" Grimes laughed out loud. "Beamer is protecting us helpless folks from road agents."

"You don't seem too worried," Cord said.

"Nor should I be. We're carrying a little something in the box, but any fool knows there's richer pickings on the lines serving the gold camps."

Cord skipped the conversation and the dried apple-pie dessert to hurry outside and tend his horse. While Grimes hitched a new team, Valerie and Beulah scrubbed off their accumulation of dust and grime despite knowing they'd be filthy again after five minutes back on the coach.

The road past the swing station seemed smoother, or maybe they were getting accustomed to being bounced about. The Smolleys were silent, nursing their unhappiness, as everyone got into the rhythm of a long, tiring ride. Valerie tried to nap, resting her head on Cord's shoulder. Cord half dozed himself.

The sharp, unmistakable crack of a carbine

brought Cord fully alert. The coach lurched suddenly and stopped, piling the passengers into a jumble on top of one another. Cord heard Billy Grimes cursing. A pistol exploded right over his head and Cord saw Beamer jump off the coach roof, run toward the side of the road, turn and fire wildly in the direction of the coach and disappear into a stand of trees.

"Get down to the floor!" Cord shouted at Valerie and the Smolleys. He heard two more rifle shots, followed by an almost instant echo. The gun had been fired from some distance.

Cord tore off the curtain on the far side of the coach, away from the sound of the gunfire. He poked his head out the window and looked up toward the driver's seat. Billy Grimes was sprawled on the seat, holding one hand over a blood-soaked section of his shirt near the shoulder. One of his fingers was actually pushed into a bullet hole as if he were the little Dutch boy holding back the tide with his finger in the dike. Cord climbed out the window and onto the driver's seat next to Grimes. "Stay where you are," he cautioned the other passengers.

Cord reached for the Springfield he'd thrown up to Grimes earlier. He ducked low on the coach seat and scanned the horizon.

"Ambush," Billy Grimes said through clenched teeth. "Somebody shot the lead mule. Dropped the dumb animal like a sack of wheat. The minute it happened, Beamer, that cur, pulled one of his Colts and shot me through the shoulder. The son of a bitch meant to kill me. When he botched the job, he jumped off the stage and run off."

Grimes was still weakly hanging on to the reins with the hand not occupied plugging up his wound. There was no need because neither team nor coach was going anywhere. Two more mules were down, blood flowing out of their foreheads.

Another shot split the air and a fourth mule flopped into the dust. The shooter sure meant for them to walk the rest of the way. Cord spotted the puff of smoke that gave the ambusher's position. About one hundred and fifty yards away, on a small hill, a man wearing a blue bandanna casually reloaded a Winchester, his back propped against a low-hanging tree branch. A cayuse stood tied to a nearby bush. The man leveled the Winchester, took careful aim and squeezed off a round. Their last mule dropped in his tracks.

"That bastard is a damn fine shot," Grimes gasped. "Every round he's pulled has gone straight to the forehead."

"He's using a '73 single-shot," Cord said, putting the butt of his Springfield up to his shoulder. "Better range and accuracy than a repeater, but it slows him down some. Let's see how deadly he is when someone's returning fire."

Cord pulled off four fast rounds that kicked up dust near the sharpshooter's feet. The man on the hill reloaded, shifted his sights as if in punishment and shot Cord's Morgan. The horse whinnied once and dropped. Cord cursed and jammed more cartridges into his rifle. He aimed higher and got off two more shots, one of the bullets creasing the

tree branch that Blue Bandanna was using for a
back rest. He quickly ducked behind a tree trunk.
Cord sighted properly and waited for something
to show. No matter what it was: an arm, a leg, a
head, he was going to blow it away.

Blue Bandanna sat tight under the cover of the
tree trunk. Cord fired twice, chipping off some
bark, in the hope he could flush the bushwacker.

The coach door burst open and Ham and Beulah Smolley tumbled to the ground. They looked
around, confused. "Get back inside," Cord shouted.
They ignored his warning and rushed, in a middle-
aged hobble, toward the same stand of trees that
had swallowed Dick Beamer.

They were at the edge of the woods when
Beamer stepped into the clear, an army Colt in
each hand. He was still playing Wild Bill. "Welcome
to the fun," he said, like a character in one of Ned
Buntline's popular western melodramas. His Colts
roared. Despite the almost point-blank range, his
first shots whistled past the Smolleys. Cord desperately swung his Springfield toward Beamer. But
before he could take aim, Beamer fired again, this
time the bullets tearing into his targets. Beulah
fell immediately. The butternut dye of her home-
spun dress was stained a deep shade of red that
rapidly spread from her waist to her collar. Ham
ran another three steps before dropping to his
knees and coming to rest against a small pine. He
looked hopelessly toward Beulah and toppled over.
Even from the coach Cord could see that the
Smolleys' bodies lay inert and lifeless.

Beamer started running back toward the cover

of the trees. Cord squeezed off a careful shot. Beamer dropped, a red hole the size of a quarter where his right eye had been. He flopped face-down less than ten yards from his victims.

Cord turned again toward the hill to see Blue Bandanna astride his horse disappearing over the crest. He pumped the lever on his Springfield and threw a nothing-to-lose shot toward the bushwacker, knocking off his hat. Blue Bandanna raised his hand in a mock salute before moving over the crest and out of sight.

Cord jumped off the coach and ran toward the pine trees to confirm his fears about the Smolleys. One glance up close told him their bad luck had dogged them to the end. Valerie appeared at the stagecoach window. "Is it over?" she asked.

"Better stay inside," Cord advised. She ignored the warning to come out of the coach and hold Beulah Smolley's body. Valerie held the woman close and cried quietly.

"What the hell do you think happened here?" Cord asked Billy Grimes after he helped him down. "This was like no stage holdup I ever heard of."

"We're carrying about nine hundred dollars in greenbacks," Grimes said. Cord could see that Billy's shoulder wound was beginning to cause severe pain. "That's not enough to tempt a gang, but it's a year's wages apiece for two men. I reckon Beamer got a job with the line strictly to pull this off. Looks like the plan was to kill me after his partner stopped the coach by shooting the mules. Only Beamer was a bad shot and had worse nerves.

They probably didn't count on a passenger as good with a gun as you."

"Seems to me they never made a serious try for your strongbox," Cord said. "The man on the hill was a crack shot, but his only target was our animals. Why didn't he shoot at us? There'd be no problem taking away the money if we were dead."

"Beamer killed the Smolleys," Grimes reminded Cord.

"I think Beamer was trying to make up for turning tail by showing how ornery he could be. Killing those poor farmers didn't seem to be part of the ambush plan."

"Most of these dumb bandits don't have much of a plan," Grimes responded.

Cord wasn't satisfied. He wanted to talk to Valerie about the powerful people who seemed to frighten her. He started toward her and noticed a look of hatred appear on Grimes' face.

Blue Bandanna appeared on a far, far ridge and reined his horse. He insolently silhouetted himself against the skyline. "Give me that rifle," Grimes muttered.

"No use," Cord said. "He's sitting up there in plain sight because he knows he's out of effective range."

Cord reached for the binoculars that Grimes kept next to him on the driver's seat. He focused on Blue Bandanna's face, looking for a feature that would help identify the bushwacker should they ever meet again.

Cord saw a thin face, still partially concealed by the handkerchief. He had black hair with a widow's

peak and yellow, lifeless eyes. They were eyes
with everything on the surface, no depth, no feeling except malice and hatred. Cord had seen eyes
like that many times before in his lifetime but
never on a human being. They were the eyes
of a rattler or cottonmouth. They hid something
poisonous. They were snake eyes.

Blue Bandanna remained motionless atop his
horse on the far ridge. He seemed to be tempting
them, deliberately offering an impossible target.
What's he trying to prove? Cord wondered.

Blue Bandanna rolled his Winchester out of its
grip, raised the rifle to his shoulder, aimed it in
the direction of the coach and stood in his saddle.
A useless gesture, thought Cord. No one's accu-
rate from that distance, not even with a Winchester '73, unless he's some kind of circus trick-shot
artist. Still, better be careful.

"Get behind the cover of those pines," Cord
called to Valerie as he helped Grimes behind the
far side of the coach. She ignored him, still intent
on Beulah Smolley.

Blue Bandanna poised for a moment, standing
in his stirrups. His horse was absolutely still. Cord
saw a white puff of smoke from the rifle, a minis-
cule cloud on a cloudless day. The puff was followed almost instantaneously by a sharp crack.
The sound bounced off the nearby hills, echoing
down to Cord. Blue Bandanna raised his rifle high
after his throwaway shot, pumping his arm in
triumph. Rider and horse disappeared over the far
ridge.

What the hell does he have to be happy about?

Cord wondered. The stage kept the money and his partner is dead.

"Jesus H. Christ," Grimes shouted. There was almost a sob in his voice. "What a damn shame! What lousy luck! An impossible shot like that."

Cord jerked his head over to where Valerie had been bending over Beulah Smolley. Two female figures were on the ground now. Valerie's body sprawled across Beulah's. The lower half of her face had completely disintegrated from the rifle slug that had slammed flush into her mouth.

6

Cord dug into the soft earth near the stand of pines to make shallow graves for the Smolleys and Valerie. Billy Grimes watched him, cursing his wound and Dick Beamer.

"Leave that skunk up top," Grimes said. "There could be some posters on him."

Cord filled in the graves. The soft wind brushing through the pines provided the service.

"This is a good place to be buried," Grimes said. "Peaceful and green ."

"There are no good places," Cord replied. He knocked the heels off his boots for the fourteen-mile hike back to the swing station.

"I'm leaving you with the water," he told Grimes. "I'll tell the station master to send a wagon for you. They should be here tomorrow. I hope your snuff holds out."

"Sounds like you ain't going to be there by the time they haul me back," Grimes said.

"No, I'm going on."

"What if there's a reward on this desperado you plugged? Where do I send your share?"

"Keep it for the next time we meet," Cord said. He didn't like leaving forwarding addresses.

"Then take your pick of the mustangs in the remuda," Grimes said. "Tell the station master Grimes said it was okay. You saved my life. That should be worth a half-broke horse to the company."

Cord put his saddlebags over his shoulder and headed toward the swing station. He kept a brisk pace of a mile every fifteen minutes that got him there in three hours.

"I never knew Grimes to give away company property before," the station master grumbled. "Are you sure that shot didn't crease his skull?"

"Maybe it did at that," Cord said. "Grimes said something about retiring to a swing station like this one."

"Not here he won't!" the station master exploded. "I'd rather go through another Indian war." He thrust a greasy scrap of paper toward Cord. "I'll take a receipt for that horse."

Cord cut out a dappled gray mustang with three white stockings. He didn't care for mustangs. They were the descendants of Arabian horses brought to America in the sixteenth and seventeenth centuries by Spanish conquistadors. Hundreds of years of roaming free had made mustangs unpredictable mounts. He would have preferred a rugged Appaloosa or even the lightly built Morgan he had been riding. But his choice was the gray or shank's mare. On the road to Denver, Cord learned the mustang had a nasty habit of turning his head to nip at his rider.

Cord felt no urgency to reach his destination. The identity of Valerie's employer had been lost with her death. Cord's saddlebags were always filled with books. He rode slowly, reading, when the gray would let him, about the findings of a young Austrian doctor, Sigmund Freud. A lot of it struck him as just good common sense, some foolishness and some pure genius. The genius part was in seeing the things that everyone else had missed.

Autumn had turned the corner in the Rockies. The fluttering aspen leaves were painted in their brilliant death masks. An occasional surge of cold air brushed Cord's face leaving behind an icy fragrance. The cloudless sky was the color of his faded jeans. When he rode past the scattered shacks on Denver's outskirts, he was almost sorry.

Cord entered the town created in 1858 by prospectors turned land speculators because they anticipated a gold rush. Miners and railroad workers, pockets bulging with wages, filled the hotels, saloons and whorehouses that lined every street. Denver was the liveliest spot between St. Louis and San Francisco.

Cord usually liked to ease into a town, stay in the background, but this time he wanted to be easy to find. Valerie's boss might come looking for him when the Crestview stage didn't arrive on schedule. Besides, his pockets bulged with prize money and there was the chance he could make some more. Cord knew his life was too unpredictable to make investments or savings worthwhile. This was an opportunity to enjoy the luxury that Denver had to offer.

He checked in at the Brown Palace, the fanciest and best-known hotel and saloon in Denver. He had the best chance here for being recognized as Cord Diamondback. The Brown Palace was also the most likely place he would meet an old eastern acquaintance who remembered him as Christopher Deacon.

After stowing his gear in his room, Cord made an appearance in the saloon. He found a comfortable spot in one corner, hooked the heel of one of his new boots over the low brass rail and surveyed the huge room through the sixty-foot mirror hanging on the back wall.

More than a hundred men crowded the long marble bar, their glasses clanking against the walnut top. Pear-shaped gas globes illuminated the area near the bar so a man could see what was in his drink. The light was dim in the back of the saloon and the air hazy from the smoke of cigars. A few men who couldn't find elbow room at the bar leaned against the marble columns that rose, like pillars in a Roman temple, from floor to ceiling. Brass spittoons beside each column, one for at least every four gents, were built knee high, so even a drunk couldn't miss.

"Empty seat, mister," the poker dealer at a table near Cord said, waving to an open chair. Cord shook him off. If he ran a few good hands, some sore loser might make trouble. Cord felt he

could handle the trouble, but not the attention it
would bring. He wanted to be easy to find, not
advertise.

A fat deputy waddled through the saloon every
half hour, smiling and friendly, but cradling a
shotgun in his heavy arms. Cord realized the Brown
Palace management must be paying off the sheriff
to get special patrol service. The deputy noticed
Cord and examined his handsome, disturbing face
as if he planned to run back to the sheriff's office
to finger through old wanted posters.

Cord checked the men in the brightly lit area
near the front of the saloon. He saw no one he
recognized. He squinted to make out the faces of
the men sitting at the tables in the rear. His eyes
scanned past one table, then returned. They rested
on one cardplayer.

Cord took two steps forward, pushing the smoke
out of his face. Anger rose in him like a prairie fire
out of control. He slammed his beer glass down
hard on the walnut bar, making the bartender
look up in surprise.

Cord willed his anger down. Being out of control was dangerous and he needed his judgment
clear. His hatred still smoldered just beneath the
surface, ready to burst into flame.

It was him! At the last table, peering from behind a poker hand, were those same yellow eyes
that belonged to the man who had ambushed the
stage and killed Valerie. Snake Eyes.

7

Cord unconsciously flexed the fingers on his gun hand. He walked slowly toward Snake Eyes' table, the hand trailing near his holster. He felt his skin tingle as his blood rose.

Cord focused on the table, blocking out everything else in the saloon. He cased the other players. No one appeared to be a particular friend of Snake Eyes. Cord could concentrate on the bushwacker. One on one.

Snake Eyes threw down his poker hand in disgust as another man raked in the pot. He still hadn't spotted Cord coming up on him. For a killer he's careless, Cord thought.

For the first time Cord saw the lower half of his face. There was no bandanna to hide behind now. His wide mouth had thick, mealy lips that he licked constantly. The nose was razor-thin with pinhole nostrils that looked like they couldn't take in enough air. His chin receded sharply until it looked like it merged with his neck. A nervous tic attacked one of his cheek muscles, jumping about his face like a Mexican flea. The man with the cruelest eyes Cord had ever seen owned a weak, dissipated, cowardly face.

Snake Eyes reached for a whiskey glass with a shaking hand that spilled half the liquid before it ever reached his mouth. His thick lips trembled as he drank. He wiped his mouth with the back of his hand and looked anxiously, finally noticing Cord.

"You want me, mister?" Snake Eyes asked. His voice came at Cord in a low whine, like a dog who didn't want to be whipped.

Cord couldn't believe that this nervous spineless drunk was the same sharpshooter who coolly drilled a complete team of mules and arrogantly stood in his saddle to gun down Valerie Blake with an impossible long shot. That man had nerves that could cut diamonds. This wasn't the same person. But the eyes were identical! They were flat and yellow and glistening, the way slime glistens.

"Yes, sir," Cord said, tipping his hat. "I've got that saddle you ordered. It's outside."

"What saddle?"

"Three days ago in Crestview. You paid half, but wanted some fancy tooling. Remember? You said you'd pay the rest when I made delivery in Denver."

"You're nuts, I never ordered a saddle."

."But you were in Crestview three days ago." Cord's voice had a sudden knife edge to it that made the other men in the card game shift their chairs away from Snake Eyes.

"It happens I was here three days ago," Snake Eyes said, reaching for a drink. "And this is where I aim to be next week."

The dealer, a bearded man in a satin vest, stopped shuffling the cards to glance up at Cord. He seemed annoyed that the game had been interrupted. "George is probably right about that, mister. He's never far from booze."

"Will you personally vouch that he was here all last week?" Cord asked coldly.

The dealer averted his eyes from Cord's hard stare and shook his head.

Cord turned back to Snake Eyes. "What else do they call you, George?"

Snake Eyes' cheek twitched uncontrollably. He put his drink to his lips, dribbling whiskey across his chin and down his vest. "I'm George Bennet," he said. "My name's no secret."

The fat deputy came ambling up, his double chin creased with a professional smile. "What's the trouble here, Nat?" he asked the dealer.

"This man's rousting Bennet," the dealer said, getting his nerve back. "Something about a saddle."

The deputy shifted his body so the shotgun he cradled in the crook of his arm almost pointed at Cord Diamondback. "You got some complaint against George?"

"The Crestview stage was ambushed three days ago. Six animals and three people were killed. I think Bennet here was the bushwacker. I was trying to place him in Crestview."

The deputy nodded, his chin disappearing in folds of fat. "We got news about that on the wire. Wasn't them all long-range shots?"

"The ambusher was a real marksman," Cord said.

"And you think this man done it?" The deputy laughed. "George? Look at his hands! A man whose hands shake like that ain't no sharpshooter. What positive identification you got?"

"None," Cord admitted. "The lower half of the ambusher's face was covered by a bandanna."

The phony cordiality disappeared from the deputy's face. "I've known Bennet for almost a year," he said. "We've had a few drinks together. You got my personal word that George couldn't hit the floor with a scatter gun. You I've seen only once before, and that was when I made my last rounds a half hour ago. I pegged you a trouble-maker and I guess I'm right. You're accusing a man of triple murder and you got no evidence. Why don't you go back to the bar and leave George alone?"

Cord didn't feel threatened by the deputy, but nothing fit about George Bennet except those damned eyes. Maybe the binoculars had distorted his vision. No! The eyes were the same. But this couldn't be the same person.

"Do you have a brother, Bennet?" Cord asked, ignoring the deputy's exasperated look.

"Nope," Bennet replied, taking courage from the support of the deputy. "Got three sisters scattered around though. Maybe one of them did it." He laughed. "They're sure mean enough."

The deputy pointed his scatter gun directly at Cord's face. "I say Bennet ain't your man. If you don't stop pestering him, I'll get the sheriff down here and we'll let you cool off for a week in our jail. That'll give me plenty of time to go through old wanted posters."

Cord walked away, conscious that the men at the poker table watched his retreating back. The dealer said, "I don't know why that fella is fixed on you as a bushwacker, George, but was I you, I'd steer clear of him."

Cord remained in the saloon for another hour. He wished he'd pressed Valerie for more information about her employer. All he knew was that the man was powerful and Valerie was afraid of him. Why hadn't this powerful man started inquiries about Valerie's disappearance? Perhaps he knew. According to the deputy, the news about the stage was on the telegraph.

Cord thought he'd stay one more day, maybe trade the mustang for something better. If no one contacted him tomorrow, he'd leave Denver. The town was too big, too cosmopolitan for a fugitive. There was opportunity for Cord Diamondback but danger for Christopher Deacon.

Cord slept like a cat with an unfriendly dog in the house. One eye was never quite closed and one ear remained alert for trouble. He came awake fully alert. From the next room he heard a saloon girl and a drunken cowboy make boisterous love. He relaxed in his bed. No! Those weren't the sounds that awakened him. There was a movement outside the door to his room. Cord concentrated on the door, filtering out the giggles and moans from the next room. He heard a delicate scratch as a key was fitted into his lock. The bolt slowly turned. Cord reached for his revolver.

8

Cord kept his eye on the chair he had wedged against the door. The chair rattled slightly but held as someone applied pressure from the other side. He heard voices arguing in loud whispers. Silence. More whispers.

"Mr. Diamondback?" called a female voice.

Cord hustled away from his bed and slapped on his trousers.

The feminine voice grew more insistent. "Please open, Mr. Diamondback." Cord saw the shadows of two figures in the space beneath the door.

"Just a minute," Cord said, quickly leaving the spot where he had spoken. No point in getting blasted through the door. He placed his kerosene lamp on a small table to one side of the door and turned the wick high. He removed the chair from its wedged position and turned it over about a foot inside the room. Anyone charging into the room would be blinded for an instant and fall over the obstacle. Cord unlocked the door with his left hand, quickly stepping into the shadows cast by the room's chifferobe.

"It's open," he said, Smith and Wesson aimed at the entrance.

The door swung wide. No one entered and there was silence in the hall. Whoever's out there is waiting until he's accustomed to the light, Cord thought. He heard the female voice whisper something. The voice sounded insistent. Cord saw the toe of a cowboy boot hesitantly edge past the threshold. The barrel of a Remington poked in at doorknob level, reflecting the light from the kerosene lamp.

Cord stepped out of the shadows. Standing to one side, he grabbed the barrel of the Remington with his left hand and yanked forward with all his strength. A man's husky shape came hurtling into the room, out of control but still hanging on to the other end of the rifle. The man's knees crashed into the overturned chair. He lost his balance and his grip on the rifle at the same time, awarding Cord sole possession of the weapon. The intruder pitched into the bedpost, sprawled to the floor and landed with his back supported by the bed. He moved his right hand toward one of the two pistols on his gun belt. Cord, still holding the Remington by the barrel, swung it in a wide arc, creasing the man across the temple with the gunstock. The crack of hard wood on hard skull sounded like a hammer driving home a nail. The man slumped over with a groan.

"Jorge is not going to appreciate that when he wakes up," Cord heard a woman say. "Jorge has a nasty temper. I'd be careful if I were you, Mr. Diamondback."

"Do you mind stepping into the light where I can see you?" Cord asked. He kept the Remington ready.

The woman appeared in the doorway and walked into Cord's room with a regal step as if she were headed to a coronation. She seemed about forty years old, slightly past her prime, but Cord almost gasped at her beauty. She had a perfect, oval face with high cheekbones and full lips. Her figure was slender and held stiffly as if she were at parade attention. Her eyes were ice blue and haughty. She carried herself with an aristocratic elegance that stated everything in life; beauty, money, position, power were hers by divine right.

"Jorge shouldn't be surprised by his reception when he barges into a room with his rifle out in front of him," Cord said.

"When we make someone a financial proposition, we don't expect violence for an answer," the woman told Cord. Her voice had an affected English drawing-room accent. "I'm Anna," she said. She pursed her lips when she spoke, showing Cord frown marks about her mouth. He noticed her black hair, tipped with silver, was worn completely swept back. He had found that women who kept their hair off their faces considered themselves beautiful. They saw no need to hide any feature.

"Too bad about your employee, Valerie Blake, isn't it?" Cord said.

Anna appeared annoyed. "What's Valerie done this time?"

"She's dead. Shot from ambush on the Crestview stage." Cord carefully watched her face for a reaction.

"That's regrettable," Anna said. She showed as much emotion as if someone had told her the roast was burned. "Jay will be devastated. Were they after you, Mr. Diamondback?"

"What makes you think that?"

She shrugged. "Violence breeds violence."

"No." Cord said. "Not a single shot was fired in my direction. Valerie may have been killed by accident. I can't be sure."

Anna suddenly lost interest in the ambush. "Still you came, Mr. Diamondback. Like a good servant, Valerie fulfilled her last assignment."

"Do you beat good servants?" Cord asked.

"I don't know what you mean. You're not suggesting Mr. Mellard beats his employees?"

"Jay Mellard, the railroad tycoon?"

"Financier. Railroads are just one of Mr. Mellard's many interests. Valerie is . . . was his secretary. Please come with me now to meet him."

"What does Jay Mellard want with me?" Cord asked. He hadn't forgotten that the woman planned to bring him at gunpoint.

"Didn't Valerie explain that before she . . . passed on?"

"You know how vague servants can be," Cord said.

She ignored the sarcasm. "Your legal services

are needed. I'm sure Valerie informed you that Mr. Mellard is generous to his people."

"Like Valerie?"

"She was well paid."

Cord examined the woman closely. Her coolness intrigued him. "Valerie was afraid of him," he said. "And I saw the reason. Does Mr. Mellard, the well-known financier, know that I won't let him make my decisions for me?"

For the first time Cord saw her smile, a thin, tentative crease of the lips as if she were stepping into unfamiliar territory. "You're not corruptible? I find that notion exhilarating. So will Mr. Mellard. Please explain it to him in detail when he's standing by with an open checkbook." She turned her back and walked out the door, obviously expecting Cord to follow.

He was attracted to Anna's beauty despite the approximate ten years' difference in their ages. He didn't like her affected superiority, didn't want to follow her, but he wanted to hear more about Mellard's proposition. The man had more than a thousand employees on his direct payroll, perhaps hundreds more he paid under the table. He controlled lawyers and judges. Why did he need Cord Diamondback?

Jorge groaned again. Cord tried lifting him, thought better of it and dragged the gunman out into the hall by his arm.

The woman waited outside, unconcerned by Jorge's physical distress. "He was a mistake," she admitted. "I brought him along to ensure that you'd come with me. "It's good of you to help him now."

"I'm not helping him," Cord said, sailing the gunman's hat into the hall. "I'm just getting him the hell out of my room."

She looked at Cord as if his last remark was the final insubordination and walked down the hall to the stairs, quite aware of her attractive figure. Cord stayed near the entrance to his room, damned if he would follow her. Finally she turned around. "Are you coming?"

"Only if you answer one question," Cord said. "First Mellard sent Valerie and now he sends you. Does he always use female employees to do his fetching?"

She raised an eyebrow to show surprise. "Employee? Please don't compare me with Valerie. My relationship with Mr. Mellard is much more personal."

9

"While we're waiting for Jay, would you mind putting your guns in this drawer?" Anna asked. "They make him nervous."

"Guns make me nervous too," Cord said. "Especially when other people are wearing them."

"Suit yourself," Anna said. "But Mr. Mellard won't like it."

She motioned Cord to sit at the table with her while they waited for Mellard. Both the table and accompanying chairs had been bolted to the floor to remain stable when the car was traveling over rough track. Cord remained on his feet, inspecting the car, anxious to learn as much as possible about its owner.

Mellard's custom-made Pullman coach perched on a track siding near Denver's central railyard. The furnishings inside the coach, wood-paneled walls, brocaded chairs, brass fittings, were examples of reckless overspending. The coach was the domain of a self-indulgent man.

On a wall shelf Cord noticed well-bound books by Sir Walter Scott, Robert Louis Stevenson and Alexandre Dumas. Whoever read those books liked adventure stories, he thought. On the same shelf, crammed behind the books, were recent issues of western magazines, including the *New Buffalo Bill Weekly* and the *Wild West Weekly*. The magazines hawked stories by E.C.Z. Judson, also known as Ned Buntline, and Colonel Prentiss Ingraham. Cord smiled when he thought about the lurid stories in those magazines, including a few about himself. Whoever read those magazines received an unrealistic, romanticized picture of the West.

The coach door jerked open and Jorge burst in followed by a very young man. "You're Diamondback," the young man said enthusiastically, stepping briskly to Cord and pumping his hand. "Looking at my traveling library, are you?"

The young man appeared to be nineteen or twenty. He had a slight build and unlined face. A wispy mustache unsuccessfully tried to take root on his upper lip. He wore a frock coat with a beaver collar in what Cord guessed was an effort at maturity.

"I'm Jay Mellard." The young man continued to pump Cord's hand as if he were trying to raise water from a deep well.

"I expected you to be older," Cord said.

Mellard frowned. "Why's that?"

"I heard you were one of the ten richest men in the United States."

Mellard grinned easily. "You must mean my father. He died six months ago. We're still not clear on everything in the estate, but I'd guess he was one of the five richest."

"Whatcha do with my rifle?" Jorge growled. He stood near the coach door playing with the purple knob on his forehead where Cord had belted him. The gun butts on his revolver were reversed in the holsters and the holsters tied down. Jorge fancied himself a real *pistolero*.

Mellard turned back to his employee. "Please forget about that incident, Jorge," he said. He smiled again at Cord as if asking him to forget it too.

"He took my rifle."

"I'll get you a new one."

Jorge considered this and shook his head. "It's not the same."

Cord would have to watch his back from now on.

Cord noticed that Mellard wore a Harvard class ring. He felt a sudden sense of loss. He had left Harvard Law School voluntarily, but now he could not even admit that it had ever been part of his life. He would have loved chatting to a fellow alumnus about life in the yard. Judging from Mellard's apparent age, he might have been an entering freshman when Cord was in law school. They might have shared a table in the library. Cord longed to ask the young man about former friends and old teachers. He smiled at himself. After all these years, he wanted a bull session about Harvard!

"Jorge's told me about Valerie," Mellard said, shattering Cord's reverie. "A terrible tragedy. She was a dear friend and valued employee. I'll deeply miss her. Can you provide any details?"

Cord filled them in on the ambush, thinking that Jay Mellard did not fit the ogre image that Valerie had given him. Why was she so terrified of this man? Could he have given her those bruises on her back? Perhaps there was a side to him that Cord hadn't seen yet.

"Tell me something about the assignment," Cord said.

Mellard inspected Cord thoughtfully. "What's the most important commodity in the West?" he asked unexpectedly.

"Water," Cord answered.

Mellard looked disappointed, like a teacher whose students do well on a quiz he expects them to fail. "That's right," he said. "Most people think it's gold." His disappointment faded and he was once again full of enthusiasm. "I can see where you get your reputation. You're sharp, just like in that dime novel about your exploits. What was it called? *Six-Gun Justice*, I believe."

"I read the book," Cord said. "There were very few facts in it." Cord didn't add that he had enjoyed reading about himself even if most of the material was fiction.

"No matter," Mellard said. "Men like you and Buffalo Bill, and a few others, are the real heroes of the West."

"Please get on with it, Jay," Anna said. "If you

keep praising Mr. Diamondback, he'll only raise his rates."

"Of course, Anna." Mellard pulled a map of Colorado from the table drawer. "My railroad's in a dogfight with the Union Pacific, the Central Pacific and every other line willing to bribe a congressman for preferential treatment on right-of-way. All of us piled up debts getting out here. Laying track costs up to thirty thousand dollars a mile. Now, we're all riding the same caboose, looking for revenue to pay off bond holders."

"Don't give him the overview, Jay," Anna said. "Just tell him what you want done."

Cord wondered about their relationship. Was she Mellard's mistress? She was about twenty years older, but some young men preferred older women. Made them feel mature. But would a mistress speak so sharply in the presence of a stranger?

Mellard grinned at Cord. "She thinks she knows how everything should be done." He pointed to a map. "I want to build a spur line to a valley about two hundred miles from here." His finger traced a line to a spot northwest of Denver. "Between here and there is all rough country with mountains, gorges, rivers and melting snow from the high country. This track is going to be more expensive than what we spent coming over the Great Divide."

"Why build it then?" Cord asked.

"Same reason the railroad does everything. Commerce. There's sweet grass in Sheltered Valley. The steers are fat and the meat's tender. The soil's rich and black and the farmers are Amish folks who know how to use it. Up in the hills above the

valley, miners are working a good, rich vein. A
spur line can freight the crops and cattle and gold
to market. We need that freight revenue."

"I still don't see why you need me," Cord said.
"I'm no surveyor."

Mellard pounded his fist on the map in youthful
exasperation. "The people up there are killing
each other over water! Apparently there's not
enough to go around. The fighting's so damn heavy
nobody's raising crops or tending the cattle. I
can't spend millions laying track to a trouble spot.
I may be president of the railroad, but my board of
directors think's I'm a snot-nosed kid who inher-
ited the job from his rich daddy. They're aching
for me to make a big mistake so they can boot me
out."

"What exactly do you want me to do?" Cord
asked.

Mellard clapped Cord on the back, obviously
believing they had a deal. "Some of the folks that
way have heard about Cord Diamondback. They
know your reputation for being impartial and have
agreed to abide by any decision you make. Go up
there, find out which group is the strongest. I'm
looking for long-range stability because a rail line
can develop that entire section of the state. We'll
decide things in the favor of the group that has the
most power. I don't want this dispute breaking
out every few years."

"You have a dispute breaking out right here,"
Cord said.

"What do you mean?"

"I won't go up there with a preconceived notion

of how the problem will be settled. That's not the way I work."

Mellard glanced over to Anna, then apparently decided to exercise his executive authority. "Mr. Diamondback, I'm paying you. That's the way I'm telling you to work."

"Get another judge," Cord said, moving toward the door.

Jorge stepped in front of the coach door to block Cord's way. The *pistolero*'s right hand slid toward the gun in his tied-down holster. Cord could clearly see Jorge's wrist twist inward as he went for a reverse pullout. Cord's arm shot forward, looking like the blur of a hummingbird's wings. His hand covered Jorge's before the gun cleared his holster.

"Try to pull that and you'll blow off your foot," Cord said. Jorge's eyes stared into Cord's with a mixture of hate and fear. His left hand inched toward his other revolver. Cord got there first, yanking the gun out of Jorge's holster. "That's one problem with wearing them backward," he said. Jorge shrugged and relaxed.

"I told you Diamondback wouldn't be suitable," Anna said.

"Nonsense." Jay Mellard's face broke into a youthful grin. "He's the man of action I'm looking for. Diamondback, you're just like that novel about you. Please don't go. I'm willing to negotiate the terms."

"Fine, we can negotiate the price, time, benefits, but not the decision."

"I mean negotiate your fee," Mellard replied.

"You can settle the dispute any way that will bring stability to the valley."

"There'll be no attempt to interfere?"

Mellard nodded. "How much?"

"Your note mentioned the figure of five thousand dollars," Cord said. "If both sides have already agreed to accept my decision, that seems a fair figure. This job should be one of my easier ones."

Jay Mellard exchanged a look with Anna. "There is one other problem. Come to my home for dinner. We can discuss it there."

"We can discuss it now," Cord said.

"I'll tell him," Anna said. "Neither the farmers nor ranchers have any water right now, except for what's in their wells. The miners in the hills above the valley have dammed all the streams. They're using the water for sluicing gold ore."

"I can clear that up when I get there," Cord said.

"It may not be that easy."

"I thought both parties have agreed to abide by my decision."

"The farmers and ranchers have."

"But not the miners?"

Jay Mellard looked uncomfortable. "They said they'd hang anyone who tried to take down their dams."

10

"The food must be old hat for you, Cord," Mellard said, passing a silver plate heaped with Buffalo steak and collard greens. "But I wanted a taste of the real West."

"I can see you enjoy roughing it," Cord answered, as a manservant dressed in the only tuxedo in Colorado poured the wine.

The dining room in Mellard's ten-room mansion was hung with woven tapestries. The mahogany dining table rested on a sixteenth-century Tabriz-design rug. Anna gave the manservant directions in French.

"Did you know Buffalo Bill?" Mellard asked eagerly. "What kind of man is Wyatt Earp?"

"Never met either man," Cord said. "I saw Cody's show once. He gave the customers their money's worth. It's well known that Earp's a lawman for profit. The only reason he wears a badge is so he can control the gambling in town. That's why he keeps moving from place to place. Earp wears out his welcome."

"Mr. Diamondback seems to be trying to dull your enthusiasm, Jay," Anna said.

Cord looked at her with appreciation. Anna didn't miss much. She was intelligent and perceptive as well as beautiful. He had found Jay Mellard naive about the West and was trying to bring him in touch with reality.

"They are great men," Mellard said, apparently not offended by Cord's appraisal. "As are you, Cord."

"Mr. Diamondback hides his greatness well," Anna said.

" 'Some have greatness thrust upon 'em,' " Cord quoted.

Anna raised her wineglass toward him in an amused gesture. "It's time we let Mr. Diamondback retire," she said, rising from the table. "I believe he wishes to leave early." She picked up a candelabrum and escorted him to his room. "I want to talk to you later," she said at his door.

"What do you wish to discuss that didn't get said over dinner?"

"The chance for you to earn a five-thousand-dollar bonus."

"I'm always willing to talk about money," Cord said. "But I have a commission."

"This won't interfere in what you're doing for Jay. In fact, he'll be pleased."

"Then tell me about it now."

"Later," Anna said as she hurried away.

When his door opened later that evening, Cord glanced at the gilt-faced clock on his nightstand. Three hours had passed. He watched Anna approach his bed. She held her candelabrum high as she peered down at him, the tallow dripping onto the pillow near his face. A huge multistoned diamond ring on her right hand reflected the candlelight in fiery tones of blue and gold.

"I'm glad you agreed to stay," she said. "You'll find this much more comfortable than the hotel." She sat on the bed, delicately lifting the hem of her blue quilted robe.

"Apparently both establishments have room service," Cord answered. "Now, tell me how I can earn another five thousand."

"I'm not as insensitive as you seem to think," Anna said. "Both Jay and I are very upset about Valerie's murder. When you're in Sheltered Valley, I want you to try to find her killer. If you do, you'll earn a five-thousand-dollar bonus."

"What makes you think the killer would be anywhere near that area?"

"Logic," Anna answered. "I suspect the stage was ambushed to prevent you from reaching Sheltered Valley. If that's true, the killer may be up there to try again."

"Makes sense," Cord admitted. "But that's not enough."

"I beg your pardon?"

"That's not enough of a reason to bring you into my room in the middle of the night. Why couldn't you make this offer in front of Jay? Why didn't he make it?"

Anna's perfectly oval face crinkled in a thoughtful frown. "Jay's still young and inexperienced. When his father died he was thrust into a business career. There are so many things for him to think of. Sometimes he finds it overwhelming. The results of this decision to bring a rail line into Sheltered Valley could shape his success or failure. He's crowded everything else out of his mind."

"So you're looking out for the poor little rich boy, is that it? You're acting as his conscience because he's thoughtless?"

"You don't phrase things diplomatically, do you Cord?" Anna leaned over the bed and placed her hand on the blanket right over his crotch. Despite himself, he felt his penis springing to life. "That's right," she said, rubbing her hand along the length of his hardness. Her face was still cool and haughty as if she were giving a servant a small present on Christmas.

Cord took her hand away. "Not tonight," he said. "I don't deserve the honor."

Anna's lips creased in the tiniest of smiles. "You can be droll sometimes, Mr. Diamondback." Her quilted robe was held by four mother-of-pearl buttons. She unfastened the buttons one by one as if she had an eternity.

Cord saw a challenge in her cool and distant face. He wondered what lay beneath the mask. Obviously she felt tenderness toward Jay. What else? Beneath the aristocratic manner and haughtiness, what else? What caused her to seek sex with an almost total stranger? Suddenly he wanted to find out.

Anna wore nothing under her robe. Her body was sleek and slim as that of a twenty-year-old virgin. Her breasts were small and firm and pink, centered by red nipples that stood out like tiaras. She had a small waist that curved in sharply almost as if the bottom rib had been removed. Her black pubic patch grew in the midst of alabaster-white skin like an oasis on desert sands.

Anna flung the blanket from the bed, uncovering Cord's body. His penis was fully extended, standing straight from his horizontal body like a lighthouse on a rocky shore.

"It's customary for a gentleman to remove all his clothes in the presence of a naked lady," she said.

"I catch colds so easily," Cord answered. He had no intention of removing his shirt. A woman like Anna couldn't be trusted with the secret of Christopher Deacon.

She grinned, sat on the bed and rolled his penis between the palms of her hands as if she were crackling the tobacco leaves of a fine Havana cigar. She bent over Cord and took his penis into her mouth, gently sucking. He could feel her tongue working on his shaft, fluttering, licking, teasing. Her head bobbed up and down as she swallowed more of his penis. One of her hands slid down to his ball sac and she scratched, none too gently, at his testicles with her long fingernails. Cord felt his semen bubbling to the surface.

"You think this will make me more willing to cooperate with Jay?" he asked.

"I expect to get something out of it for myself," Anna replied.

Cord reached his hand toward her crotch. Still sitting, Anna spread her legs wide to accommodate him. He slipped one finger inside her. Her vagina was wet.

"Yes," she said, making the word seem like a command.

Cord moved another finger inside her and spread them in opposite directions.

"Yes," she hissed louder.

Her mouth attacked Cord's penis with new determination. His semen surged to the tip in a small eruption, spilling across her lips. A few drops dribbled across her cheeks. Anna raised her little finger and pushed the semen back into her mouth as delicately as if she was cleaning up errant gravy.

Cord was still rock hard. Anna pulled her mouth from his penis and kneeled on the bed. She straddled him and lowered her dewy vagina onto his shaft, sinking down until their pubic hairs tangled. Cord watched his penis disappear into her like a nail being driven into a two-by-four. His hands reached up and covered her aristocratic breasts. The hard nipples were still cool to the touch.

She waited for a few seconds, gently rocking until she was comfortably settled. She raised her body until only the head of Cord's penis was still inside her, stayed suspended for an instant, and then brought her body crashing down, again burying his shaft deep inside her. She repeated the maneuver several times until he understood.

She's posting! he thought, amused at the idea. She's riding me the same way she'd ride a horse.

Anna raised her body again. Cord thrust his hips upward in the same rhythm, keeping his penis buried deep inside her. She looked at him in surprise as if the stallion wasn't properly trained.

Cord sat up so they were facing one another, his shaft still contained by her vagina. He rocked forward and placed both hands on the cheeks of her ass. He kept pushing his body forward until she was forced over on her back, landing them in the classic missionary position.

"Wait," Anna said as he moved his hands down to her thighs, spreading her legs further apart.

Cord pumped into her, working hard.

"Wait, dammit," she said again, but her hips humped up to meet his thrusts.

Cord continued relentlessly pumping harder. Anna's face lost its haughty coolness and contorted with pleasure. He felt her opening beneath him, unlocking the chains to her real emotions. Her fingers grasped the cheeks of his ass. He could feel the coldness of her diamond ring digging into his skin.

Her legs clamped around his back. *"I'm coming,"* she almost screamed. Her vagina sputtered and rolled like water at a full boil. "Come too," she gasped.

Cord kept up his assault, working right through her orgasm.

"No more," she said, but she matched him motion for motion.

"My God, I'm coming again," Anna said. There was a sense of wonder in her voice.

Cord finally abandoned his own control, like taking the top off a tightly screwed mason jar. He felt his semen boiling to the top, hissing and steaming into her. Anna looked up at him, her icy eyes melting, her haughty face tender. She covered his face with small kisses.

As they lay together Cord could feel the heat pouring out of her as if she was a banked fire.

"I feel as if I've just had greatness thrust upon me," Anna said playfully. Her eyes were heavy-lidded with a sated look, like a cat drowsy from too much cream. "Were you always this good?"

" 'Some men achieve greatness,' " he quoted again, laughing.

She pushed hair from his forehead so she could look into his dark eyes. "When you finish the assignment in Sheltered Valley, I want you to come back here. I'll make Jay find something suitable for you."

"That would be awkward," Cord said.

Anna raised herself up on one elbow. Beads of sweat still clung to her small breasts. "Awkward? Why?"

"Being a paid lover to my employer's mistress is too sophisticated for me."

Anna let out a most unaristocratic giggle. "You think I'm Jay's mistress?"

"Back at the Brown Palace you told me about

your close personal relationship," Cord said. "And I've seen the way you order him around."

"Naturally." Anna laughed. "The way any mother orders her son. Not that Jay listens. He's most headstrong."

"Your Jay's mother?"

Anna Mellard nodded. "His father married me when I was seventeen. We built his financial empire together."

"Then you must own stock in the railroad."

"Of course. They're all nonvoting shares I'm afraid. Jay runs the line." She snuggled next to him again. "Now will you come back when the job is over?"

"Anna, do you seriously think I could be a paid lover?"

She sighed and kissed him on the mouth. "I suppose not. But if I didn't have Jay to look after, I'd follow you all over Colorado."

Cord rose early in the morning and rode his mustang to the stock pens on the outskirts of town. The gray, plus fifty dollars, bought him an Appaloosa with a dotted patch of white hair over his rump. At the general store he bought trail supplies and a warm buffalo robe for the two-hundred-mile ride to Sheltered Valley. He set the Appaloosa on the trail before the Mellards sat down to their breakfast.

Fifty miles in front of Cord on the Sheltered Valley trail, three men finished a camp breakfast of beans and bacon. The men's worn clothes and poor mounts showed they were used to lean times and rough going. Their hard faces and hungry eyes revealed that they were ready to do anything to change their luck. They glanced fearfully at a fourth man as he approached the small campfire and spilled his coffee into the flame. The fire hissed as the liquid hit the burning embers.

"Get your asses moving," he said softly. "I didn't hire you to lay around camp all day. We only have a day's jump on Diamondback."

"When you hired us in Denver, you didn't say you wuz a general and we wuz privates," one of the three men replied. He was short and cocky, like a banty rooster hopping around the barnyard looking for something to peck.

The man stopped and fastened the banty rooster with a stare. "Do as you're told, or make a play right now," he said, still speaking softly. "That goes for all three of you." He folded his arms in front of him, far away from his gun belt.

The men glanced at one another and rose quickly, dousing the campfire and rolling their blankets. They threw their saddles on their horses and cinched them tightly. The men groused but always moved fast when he spoke. His voice was a soft whisper and this was the first time he said anything directly threatening, but they moved fast just the same.

Yesterday, their first day on the trail, he had demonstrated his skill with a rifle. He had made impossible shots and bet he could repeat them. No one had taken his bets. There was something about the man's eyes that made them believe taking his money might be dangerous.

"Jes who is this Diamondback fella?" the banty rooster asked.

The man said nothing. His eyes followed the men as they mounted, ready to leave camp. The eyes were bright and inhuman. They seemed to sizzle at the mention of the name Diamondback. Whoever this Diamondback fella was, he was in for a horrible shock.

11

The explosion roared and ricocheted against the surrounding hills like a man-of-war broadsiding an enemy ship. Cord reined in his Appaloosa and scanned the horizon. Two hills away he sighted a thin, wavy line of black smoke already being lifted and scattered by mountain winds. Cord dug his spurs in his horse and headed for the smoke at a fast gallop.

At the crest of the first hill Cord saw two wagon-wheel ruts that cut about six inches into the earth. He set the Appaloosa following the crude road because he knew it must lead to the mining camp above Sheltered Valley. According to Mellard, the miners were going to be the most difficult group to persuade. Cord believed in tackling the toughest problem first.

The smell of burning sulfer, sharp and pungent like an aged cheese, drifted against Cord's nose.

He kicked into his horse's flank until the Appaloosa was straining to cover ground. As he topped the second hill he saw smoke billowing from a jerry-built dam constructed across a wide stream. The explosion had blasted a breech in the dam and water rushed along its old course, tumbling along a dried stream bed, headed for the valley.

Cursing miners ran toward the dam carrying buckets. They formed a ragged line from a hill of gravel to the breech, scooping the gravel into their buckets as they vainly tried to plug the hole.

The mining camp sat about four hundred yards from the dam. The campsite butted against the bottom of a small mountain like a gambler who keeps his back against the wall. Most of the buildings were rough-lumber one-room shanties. A half-dozen canvas tents, all in need of patching, and a few lean-tos made up the rest of the structures. The place had a look of impermanence as if everything could be packed up and carted off in an hour.

The miners had sunk several shafts straight down into the earth and tunneled into the side of the mountain. The perpendicular shafts had winches at the top with thick hemp ropes dangling into black holes as if someone was ice fishing in the earth. A rail track led from the tunnel to several sluices or Long Toms. The sluices were twelve-foot-long wooden troughs with a series of riffles or grooves at the bottom to catch gold as it separated from gravel. Water for the sluices was supplied by a shallow flume, or ditch, connected to the nearby dammed stream.

The miners not in the bucket brigade ran excitedly around the camp. Cord saw several miners pointing at him as he rode down the hill, but their main attention seemed to be diverted elsewhere.

Three miners dragged a woman from behind a pile of gravel.

"We found her," Cord heard one of the miners call.

"Well hold her, dammit," another miner responded.

"The bitch is slippery," the first miner complained.

The woman, tall and muscular, was giving the men all they could handle. One of the men, a thick-necked bruiser in a checkered lumberjack shirt, hit the woman hard in the face with his closed fist. The woman slumped for a moment, then broke one hand free to return his blow.

The bruiser in the lumber jack shirt released his hold on the woman and took off his cap to shield his eyes from the afternoon sun. "Anybody know that rider coming down the hill?" he asked his companions.

One of the other two miners holding the woman squinted up toward Cord. He was a short, stocky man with a pink nose that seemed to be sniffing the air like a weasel. "Naw," he said, "but let him come. Maybe he won't like it when he gets here."

The bruiser moved off to the side, giving Cord his first unobstructed view of the woman. The miners were having trouble keeping her controlled. Despite her obvious strength, she was slimly proportioned, with rounded hips that were noticeable even under her black, loose-fitting dress. She had gray-blond hair, the color of corn husks, done up in a braided bun. Her jaw jutted out, square and resolute, and her eyes were a lustrous blue with a spark of light that wouldn't stay put.

She dug in her heels against the miners who were plainly exasperated by her struggling. Weasel Nose clutched his hands around her dress fabric and tugged. The dress tore with a loud ripping noise and one of the woman's ample breasts spilled out. The miner let out a loud whoop and kept tugging at the material, worrying the rip, until both her breasts were bared. Some of the miners cheered.

The commotion brought all the miners to the scene, including those who had given up working on the dam. They gathered around the men struggling with the woman, staring bug-eyed at her naked breasts.

"Let me cover myself, I'm cold," the woman shouted. Her face looked more angry than ashamed. Cord thought he noticed the trace of a foreign accent.

"You should of thought about the weather before you come up here to blow our dam," the big bruiser said. "Now, we're going to see what else you got underneath that black dress."

Cord slid his Appaloosa to a stop and dismounted. He looked for someone in authority. The big bruiser seemed to be taking the lead, but he seemed too much of a bully to be respected by the miners.

The miners crowded in behind Cord with suspicious stares. He didn't see many rifles or pistols, but a few of the men carried pickaxes and shovels.

The bruiser yanked at the woman's dress, eyeing Cord as if daring him to protest. Some of the miners egged the bruiser on.

A tall miner with a stringbean body and a worried face stepped out of the crowd. "Wait a minute, Pete," he said. "That's enough. Maybe we owe Mrs. Kreitner a lesson, but we can't strip her down like she was a tart."

"She blew our dam, Charley," the bruiser told the gaunt miner. He glared at the woman. "We ain't through with you yet," he growled.

"You running things here?" Cord asked the thin miner.

The miner inspected Cord with tired eyes that looked like they never closed. "Anybody who's found a rich vein is in charge at this camp," he replied.

"If it takes pay dirt, then you sure as hell ain't honcho, Charley," a miner shouted. The others laughed, but Cord could see that Charley was liked and respected.

"I don't mean to interfere with your entertainment," Cord said, "but I'd like to talk to the man running this camp."

"You must help me," the woman pleaded to Cord.

"You know her?" Charley asked. "You came riding in here about the same time the dam was blowed. Who the hell are you?"

"He's with her," Pete said. "I saw him come out of hiding the minute we flushed her. Look in the bushes at the top of the hill. I'll bet there's a horse hidden there for her."

"I came here alone," the woman said. Her accent was very noticeable now as she spoke in excitement.

"How can you believe her?" Pete asked. "He showed up a few minutes after she set her charge."

"I had no part in dynamiting your dam," Cord said.

"That's mighty thin," Charley said.

"Maybe he's the dry-gulcher who picked off Steve and Frank yesterday," Pete offered.

"Careful," Charley said with a half smile that settled uneasily on his worried face. "I don't see how he can keep himself that busy. Besides, how many times can we lynch him?"

Cord saw the miners were excited and not prepared to listen to reason. They were angry about the dam and apparently two miners had been ambushed. They wanted to strike back, correct all their problems by hanging one man. Cord Diamondback didn't want to be that man. He knew he had to speak carefully now to convince the miners he didn't know the woman. Her chances depended on it too. If the miners believed they were together, he'd have no chance to speak in her behalf.

"I told you I acted alone," the woman said. "I never saw this man before."

If only she would shut up! The more she protested, the more the miners believed she was lying.

Cord started to say, "I just rode in to—"

"Bullshit," someone swore. Cord heard the sound of something hissing through the air, traveling at tremendous speed. The hissing sounded like a malicious whisper. He turned quickly to hear the whisper's message. Too late. The whisper became a roar that blotted out his senses as the blade end of a shovel smashed across the base of his skull. Darkness, total and absolute and empty of life, absorbed him.

12

Pain nudged Cord awake. He felt as if someone had put his head in a wine press and was turning the screw. Pressure against his chest made it difficult for him to breathe. His hair felt damp and sticky, matted with partially dried blood. Cord tried lifting his hand to assess the damage to his skull and realized that both his arms were tied.

He dangled in space, turning slowly, like a kite caught in a tree. He stretched his legs to bring them in contact with the ground, but somehow the earth had given way beneath him.

Only Cord's head and shoulders were above ground. The rest of his body hung suspended inside one of the perpendicular shafts the miners had dug to reach bedrock. He was tied to a harness attached to one of the winches erected over the shaft. The harness wrapped under his arms and tightened across his chest, making him look like a calf that was hogtied for branding.

He opened his eyes. He couldn't feel anything in his hands or arms as the tight ropes cut off circulation. He looked around at the miners crowded around the shaft until he located Charley. Charley seemed to be the only man willing to listen to reason. The first thing he had to do was find out what they planned to do next.

"I'm glad I didn't come on a holiday," Cord said. "These festivities are all I can stand."

Charley looked apologetic. "Don't wiggle too much. That pit you're dancing over is sunk a good eighty-five feet and the lock on this winch is known to be a mite touchy."

"You might be making a mistake sending me down there," Cord said. "There could still be some gold at the bottom of this shaft. What if I find a rich vein and file a claim?"

Charley and a few other miners laughed. "You got sand, but you're headed downstairs just the same."

"Don't I get a chance to explain what I'm doing here?" Cord asked.

Charley checked with the other miners and shook his head. "You had a short trial while you were out. Miners' court."

"Who conducted my defense?" Cord asked.

Charley scratched his head. "Nobody wanted to take your side. Half of us think you helped Gretchen Kreitner set the dynamite and the other half think you're the bushwacker who's been plaguing us the last few days. The verdict was unanimous.

You're being coyoted. In case you don't know mining, we lower men down shafts on winches so they can work bedrock. Only we plan on sending you down a touch faster than normal. First, we thought you might want to see what happens to your woman friend."

"I told you, I don't know her," Cord said. His head still throbbed.

"Then you won't mind what we do to her," Charley said. "I'm not in favor of harming women, but miners' court decided. What the hell, she knocked a hole in our dam that'll take a week to fix."

"Let me free," Cord heard Gretchen say. He turned his head toward the sound of her voice. She was tied, facedown, inside the wooden walls of one of the sluices. The ropes prevented her from raising her head more than a few inches. Gretchen's dress had been entirely torn from the upper half of her body. Her breasts crushed against the gravel and sediment resting on the riffled bottom of the sluice. Pete stood near the wooden boards that temporarily prevented water from flowing from the flume into the sluice.

"Are you watching, Diamondback?" Charley asked. He nodded toward Pete, whose ugly face beamed with a giant smile. "You feel this is necessary, Pete?" The bruiser shook his head eagerly. "Then let her rip," Charley said.

Pete lifted out the two boards that held back the water from the sluice. The water rushed through the trough, tumbling small rocks and sediment before it. The rocks and sand cascaded across

Gretchen's head, shoulders and breasts. Water filled in the bottom of the sluice, covering her face and nose. Gretchen sputtered and gasped as she lifted her face out of the water as far as her bonds would allow, exposing her breasts to more battering from the tumbling rocks.

"Charley, you can't be enjoying this," Cord said. "Put a stop to it before you kill that woman."

The miner looked at him angrily. "She used enough powder to blast another Grand Canyon. Ain't her fault we can plug the dam up in a week. Lucky for us she don't know where to set a charge."

Gretchen's neck muscles were obviously tiring because she was straining to keep her head out of the streaming water. Cord couldn't help admiring her because she hadn't once pleaded or begged. There was still a defiant glare in her eyes.

Cord said, "Charley, I know the miners are having problems with the valley people now. What do you think conditions will be like if you kill this woman?"

Charley looked at him oddly. "How come you know about our problems?"

"I was hired to find answers that everyone, including the miners, can live with," Cord said. "What you're doing today is ruining the last chance for a peaceful settlement."

"You talk good," Charley said, "but it don't look like you're in a position to help anybody." He left Cord and walked toward the sluice. "Go easy," he told Pete. "Miners' court decision was that we give her a lesson she can take back to her farmer friends in the valley. We don't drown women."

All the miners were hypnotized by the sight of Gretchen's bare breasts bobbing like corks in a lively stream. With Charley over at the sluice no one paid attention to Cord Diamondback. He began to swing his body, using his legs to build momentum. If he could develop a wide enough arc, he could swing his legs up to ground level. His hands would still be tied, but he would be on solid earth. He would worry about his hands later. One problem at a time.

Cord swung high, his legs barely grazing the surface. Next swing should do it. He bent his knees and tucked his legs for the final kip-up.

"Hey, Charley," a miner shouted. "I thought you was keeping an eye on that stranger. He's using our winch like it's a backyard swing."

Pete looked up and scowled. "Miners court wasn't so generous with him," Pete said. "I think it's time he saw the bottom." He raced to the winch and kicked the lock with his boot. The wooden wheel screeched as the rope unwound. Cord plummeted straight down toward the bottom, eighty-five feet away.

13

Cold, dank air slapped Cord's face as he hurtled toward the bottom, picking up speed as he fell. His effort to swing out of the shaft had left his body in a slightly forward position and he thought he'd probably hit on his knees and chest.

On what? Bedrock cut jagged by miners' pick-axes most likely.

A few men had survived falls from similar heights. But not many landing on that kind of surface. What if he did survive? Surely his legs and probably the bones in his chest would be broken. His hands would still be tied behind his back. He would die anyway, but more slowly and painfully. For the first time in his life, Cord fleetingly thought that death might be preferable to survival.

No! Survival meant hope. He tried to relax completely. He had heard that some people survived falls from great heights because their bodies were relaxed when striking the ground.

Cord's body snapped and jerked as the winch rope suddenly tightened. His shoulders scraped against the side of the tunnel, ripping his shirt. His arms felt like they were being torn out of their sockets. He bounced on the rope end a few times, then settled. He looked down. The bottom was pitch black, but his feet seemed only a few inches from the ground.

Charley's voice floated down the shaft, sounding hollow and very far away, as if he were using a megaphone. "Hey, stranger, is your name Cord Diamondback?"

"Yes," Cord said. The rope end twisted and untwisted, revolving his body in circles until he became dizzy.

"We're hauling you up," he heard Charley yell down. His tone seemed reluctant. Cord felt his body being lifted to the surface. The screeching winch now sounded like music.

Two miners lifted him out of the shaft and untied his harness. Charley held out his hand as if there were no hard feelings.

"Miss me while I was gone?" Cord asked, rubbing his wrists and arms to restore circulation.

Charley pointed to another miner. "Stan here just came into camp. He saw you leaving Denver about the same time he did. You couldn't be the hombre who sniped at our camp yesterday. I don't see how you could have helped Gretchen Kreitner set the dynamite either."

"Honest mistake, right?"

"We ain't apologizing. You should know better than to come into a miners' camp and start interfering."

Cord looked over toward the sluice. Gretchen was still being bombarded by water and gravel. Her head drooped below water level to the bottom of the trough. She'd pull it back with loud gasps, but Cord saw her spunk leaving her, washed away with the ice-cold water.

"What about the woman?"

"Hell, there's no mistake there. She even admitted blowing the dam. Acts like she's even proud of doing it."

"I think you've laundered a lesson into her by now," Cord said.

"You could be right," Charley said. He cupped his hands and shouted. "Hey, Pete, you let her out of there."

"Like hell I will," Pete snarled. "If we free her now, our dam will be blown again before we get it plugged."

Cord noticed the miners looking at one another, not sure how to react. They weren't solidly behind Pete, but apparently were reluctant to stop him. Damn! There didn't seem any other way except taking a hand. If the farmers found out he'd stood by while one of their own was killed, he'd lose all credibility. They wouldn't listen to anything he had to say. Maybe he could do something without making a fuss. Cord walked quickly to the flume and replaced the two wooden boards, shutting off the flow of water.

"Who the hell do you think you are?" Pete roared. He swung a ham-sized right hand that whistled past Cord's face. Cord let Pete's swing carry his body closer. He smelled of freshly dug earth. Cord unleashed a solid right hand that caught the miner in the right eye, turning the lid purple. Pete covered his eye with his right hand, allowing Cord to dance over to his unprotected side and pepper Pete's body with short, sharp punches.

Cord popped two cruel lefts to Pete's kidneys, turning the miner's face to sunset yellow. Pete keeled over to the ground in a fetal position.

Cord hurried to the sluice and unraveled the ropes that bound Gretchen. She looked at him gratefully, teeth chattering and white skin covered with goosebumps. Cord worked on the ropes that bound her legs when he heard the crunch of a boot behind him.

"Looks like one clout on the head ain't enough to satisfy you." The voice belonged to the chunky miner with the weasel nose. He was short, but the spade he carried extended his reach by six feet. The sharp metal edge of the blade hurtled toward Cord's head

Cord dropped flat to the ground. A few of the miners started toward him.

"Wait," Charley said, holding up his hand. "The odds is two-to-one already. You boys ease off. Stan told me something about this fella that makes me want to see how he handles himself."

Gretchen untied her remaining ropes. A sympathetic miner gave her his jacket, causing a few disappointed sighs.

Pete had shaken off the effects of the blows to his kidneys and rose to one knee. As the bruiser struggled to pull himself erect Cord crossed the ground to him and crashed his boot into Pete's temple. The miner's head snapped back, a dazed helpless look in his eyes. His body slumped to the ground looking as lifeless as one of the discarded piles of gravel.

"Geez, I ain't never seen Pete put down before." One of the miners whistled.

"Hell, that Diamondback fella fights dirty," a fat miner, who looked like he'd have a problem easing his body through a mine shaft, explained.

Charley nodded. "Maybe, but there's no denying that he got the job done."

The chunky miner wielding the spade glanced over to his fallen comrade. "Give it up, Ed," Charley shouted. I don't think you can stand up to Diamondback one on one."

Ed shook his head grimly. He backed away from Cord, keeping his spade moving in a steady, half-circle motion. The shovel whistled waist high, giving Cord no chance to go in under or leap over. Cord knew that miners used their spades to cut through hard-packed dirt and even chip away at rock. If he was clipped by the edge, the spade could slice through him as well. The blade hummed through the air in a steady circle.

Cord stood just beyond the cutting arc. The miner's muscled arms looked like they could keep up the motion for hours. Cord knew the other miners were watching, testing him. He had no weapons. His pistols had been removed earlier when he was knocked unconscious.

"Do something, will ya, Diamondback?" Charley called. "I don't think Ed's clock is due to run down until after midnight."

Cord retreated to a gravel pile and selected two fist-sized stones. He closed again on the miner, careful to stay just beyond the end of the whirring blade.

"Time to turn tail, Ed," Charley suggested. "I think you're about to be bombarded."

Ed kept the spade cutting through the air as if he were trimming a field full of weeds. Cord hefted one of the stones in his right hand, sighted, and hurled it toward the miner. The stone landed high on Ed's shoulder. He winced and dropped the metal end of the spade to the ground. Cord rushed forward, but Ed recovered and grazed Cord with the tip of the shovel, cutting a bloody line, straight as if it was made by a ruler, across Cord's thigh. Cord felt nothing for a moment, then a sharp pain as though he'd been stung by a hornet enveloped his upper leg.

Cord threw the second stone, but Ed easily stepped out of the way. Cord retreated to the gravel pile for more ammunition. Ed grew bolder and advanced. As Cord bent over for more stones, the miner narrowly missed clipping him across the forehead with a swing that would have scalped Cord neatly as any Sioux warrior could do.

Cord carefully measured the distance, threw his arm back and put his body weight behind another throw. The stone struck Ed on the cheek with a loud pop that probably meant a broken cheekbone. Ed dropped the spade, kneeled on the ground and cried. A few miners laughed at him.

Charley ambled up to Cord. "That was slick, Diamondback. You done just the right thing. Ed's no prize, but if you had killed that little weasel, the miners might have turned on you. Pete's different. If that fool found the Mother Lode, he'd buy trouble with it." He inspected Cord thoughtfully. "Stan tells me what you said before is true. You come here to settle the water dispute."

"Word travels fast," Cord said. "Did Stan say who hired me?"

"Don't make a helluva lot of difference," Charley replied. "As far as we're concerned, there ain't no dispute. We control the water and we're going to keep it. The farmers and the ranchers can go scratch. That goes double now that Gretchen knocked a hole in the dam and the ranchers are trying to shoot us off."

"I heard that some of your men were dry-gulched," Cord said. "What makes you think the ranchers were behind the shootings?"

"Cause they got rifles and know how to use 'em." Charley's worried face took on a new level of concern. "Besides, bushwacking ain't a farmer's style," he said pointedly at Gretchen. "They like to blow things up."

"Did you ever see anyone?" Cord asked.

"All we seen is men in the camp dropping,"

Charley answered. "Hell, it's easy to shoot from ambush around here. There's enough rocks above us to hide Custer's Seventh Cavalry, including the horses. Funny thing. The sniping would go on for a few days, stop for a week and start up again. I guess the man who was doing it would go off into town once in a while for some drinks."

Gretchen Kreitner intruded on their conversation. "I overheard your name, Mr. Diamondback," she said. "I'm grateful for your timely intervention. These fiends might have killed me."

"You'll get worse if you come up here again with dynamite in your saddlebags," Charley threatened. "Don't count on them big teats of yours to save you next time."

"The miners have no right to all the water," Gretchen answered angrily. "You're damming the stream illegally. We need water to irrigate our fields. How can you be so greedy?"

"Farmers don't know nothing about mining," Charley said to Cord. "We damn up the stream so we can placer-mine the stream bed. That's the easiest way to find gold. Then we divert the water to operate our sluice boxes. You got a firsthand demonstration on how they work. One man working a sluice box can take the place of ten miners panning for gold."

Gretchen opened her mouth to speak, obviously thought it was useless and turned toward Cord. "You can see why I tried force. These godless men won't listen to reason. Mr. Diamondback, will you escort me from this horrible place?"

"Why don't you stay for supper?" Charley asked. "We live high off the hog here. Sourdough and salt pork."

"It's time I met the people in the valley," Cord told Gretchen. He turned to Charley. "You know you can't keep the water forever," he said. "If the ranchers and farmers join forces, they can take it away from you. Before that happens, let me negotiate a settlement you can all live with."

Charley looked at Cord, apparently considering the offer. "I heard you were a fair man," he said. "But I don't see what you can do. My miners are hard set on keeping what we got. Palavering ain't going to make us take down our dams. And dry-gulching won't neither. You tell Lafe Parsons if one more miner gets shot, we'll be visiting his ranch. The way the men are feeling, they might be ready for that visit right now."

"The rancher?" Cord asked. Mellard had briefed him on the principals in the dispute.

"The no-good sonofabitch wants all the water for his cattle," Charley said. "I think he's behind the sniping."

Cord noticed that Gretchen nodded vigorously when Charley said that Parsons was no good. "A few minutes ago you thought I might be the bushwacker," Cord reminded Charley.

"Lafe Parsons is capable of anything," Gretchen interrupted.

Cord looked at her with amusement. "You're good with dynamite. Go blow up his bunkhouse." He turned to Charley. "I'm interested in the snipings. Did the shots that killed the miners come from a long distance?"

Charley nodded. "Could be. One of the miners claimed he spotted gunsmoke way off. Nobody believed him. A man would have to be a trick-shot artist to hit a target from that far."

"You say you're not interested in making any deals?" Cord asked.

"Nope." Charley set his face like he wasn't going to be persuaded no matter what was said. "We got everything we need, except enough gold."

"What about the sniper? Do you have him?"

"Course not."

"Let's say I came up here with the sniper across my saddle. Could we trade?"

"Alive?" Charley asked, scratching his chin. Cord saw that Charley was thinking there's no point in trading anything for a dead body.

"Alive."

Charley considered the proposition. "Nope," he finally said, shaking his head. "Revenge is sweet, but water is sweeter. If you got him caught, we might give you a mite of gold dust for a reward, that's all."

"How do you know he'd stay caught?" Cord asked. "I might let him go."

Charley gaped at Cord. "You'd let a murderin' bushwacker go free?"

"Why not?" Cord said. "You don't seem very interested in him."

"A man would have to be a sonofabitch to do something like that," Charley said. He smiled at

Cord. "I think you qualify. Okay, the sniper is trading material."

Cord thought back to the ambush that killed Valerie. He felt certain that the sniper operating here was the same sharpshooter. He didn't know who had hired the man or why. He just knew he'd have a chance for a five-thousand-dollar bonus and another crack at Snake Eyes.

14

"I should have set the charge lower and more to the right," Gretchen Kreitner said, frowning, as they rode past the breech in the dam caused by her dynamite charge. A few miners still poured debris into the hole, slowing the flow of water down the stream bed.

One of the miners shook his fist at her. "Bitch!" He threw a rock that fell short of their horses.

"I'll know better next time," she said. "Still, we'll have water for a few days, if Lafe Parsons doesn't steal it all for his cattle."

"Spoken like a stubborn German," Cord said. "If you try to go back, the miners will kill you."

Gretchen was able to smile in spite of her recent ordeal. "You almost guessed my accent. My parents came from Zurich, Switzerland. Most of the Amish are of Swiss origin. The majority settled in Pennsylvania. My parents came to Colorado because the Rockies reminded them of the Alps."

"That must have been a long time ago," Cord said. "Your accent is almost gone."

"That was a thousand years ago," Gretchen sighed. "Both my parents are dead now. I've buried two husbands as well. The first died of diphtheria. We tried boiling sulfer in limewater and dripping it into his nose, but the remedy didn't work. The second froze to death in a Colorado blizzard. He went to the barn to feed the stock and the snow was so blinding he couldn't find his way back to the house. He died less than one hundred yards from the front door. Less than thirty and twice widowed."

"I thought the Amish Mennonites were peaceful folks. Why do you try to settle things with dynamite?"

Gretchen's square jaw was set hard and determined. "We found this valley long before the miners scratched for gold in the hills," she said. "Those mountains to the north form a protection from the winter winds. This soil has never been turned. We can grow wheat here. If the railroad builds the spur line, we can supply Denver with fresh vegetables in the summer. This can be a good place if only we had enough water."

They followed the wagon-rut road several thousand feet down into the valley. The valley floor was flat and green with prairie grass. Cattle could graze here without moving around much to forage. Plows could cut into the rich, black earth. Cord saw why people were attracted to the place.

"Tell me about Lafe Parsons," Cord asked.

"He's as bad as the miners," Gretchen answered. "Before the miners dammed the streams, Parsons had several large ponds brimming with water. Did he share any with the farmers for their irrigation? He drove us off at rifle point. He wants to hog all the water for his steers. I'm almost glad he doesn't have any water to hog."

"Are the ponds on his land?" Cord asked.

"They're mud holes now," Gretchen answered, with a look of grim satisfaction on her face. "But most are on government land. Not that legal ownership ever bothered Lafe Parsons."

"So you'd be willing to share if Parsons would?" Cord asked, testing her.

"Of course not! There just isn't enough water for everyone. The farmers should get it all. Everyone knows you can feed more people per acre growing crops than raising beef."

"If you feel that way," Cord said, "why did you agree to abide by any decision I might make?"

Gretchen looked at Cord as if he were a simple-minded child. "Because there isn't any water at all down here. Your job is to get the water away from the miners. I'll think of some way to take it from Mr. Lafe Parsons."

Suddenly Cord reached over and grabbed the bridle on Gretchen's horse.

"What's going on?" she asked.

Cord motioned her to be silent. He guided both horses behind a small cluster of juniper bushes. From their vantage point they could see anyone traveling down the wagon-rut road, but they couldn't be seen.

"Did you hear something?" Gretchen whispered.

Cord nodded. He unholstered his Smith and Wesson and rested it across his saddle pommel. He patted the Appaloosa several times on the neck to keep him resting easy and motioned Gretchen to do the same with her horse. They heard a rider galloping hard, moving fast and recklessly, taking no precautions.

The rider crashed into view. He bent over his horse, clutching tightly to the bridle and urging the animal to greater speed. The horse's flanks were covered with sweat. The animal's head was low and his stride had lengthened as if he were close to being played out.

As the rider shot by, Cord could see his thigh was stained with blood. He went a hundred feet or so past the clump of juniper bushes concealing Cord and Gretchen when his horse collapsed or stumbled. The rider spilled into the road. His horse stayed down, not even trying to rise.

"Stay where you are," Cord told Gretchen. He dismounted and walked toward the thrown man, using bushes alongside the path for cover so the man couldn't see him approach.

The man clutched at his ankle as if it were giving him more trouble than his bloody thigh. He had a mean, hard look with thin lips that were now swearing softly.

Cord left the cover of the bushes and stepped into the path, not ten feet from where the man lay.

The man looked up at Cord and gasped. "It's you," he shouted, reaching weakly for his gun.

Cord raised his Smith and Wesson, which he had never reholstered. "Did you land on your head?" he asked. "Because you'd have to be crazy to try making a play now."

The man drew his hand away from his holster and held it in front of him, palms up, to show he wasn't holding. "I never had anything against you anyway," he said.

"I've never seen you before," Cord said. "How is it that you know me?"

"My ankle hurts like hell," the man said. "I think it's busted."

"Who are you and how do you know me?" Cord demanded. "Were you following me from Denver?"

The man's thin face looked up at Cord defiantly. "Following you? We wuz ahead of you all the time!"

Cord removed the man's pistol from his holster and inspected his fallen horse. The animal looked at Cord wildly as if appealing for help. His nostrils flared and his breathing was irregular. One of the horse's legs lay beneath him in a crazy, twisted angle. A circle of blood spotted his rib cage.

"Your horse is finished," Cord told the fallen man. The man nodded hopelessly. Cord raised his revolver and fired a single shot into the animal's ear. Gretchen turned away.

"Can you take me to where I can get fixed up?" the man asked. "I'll pay you for the trouble. There's money in my saddlebags."

"You're not going anywhere until I get some answers," Cord said.

"For Christ's sake, I'm hurt," the man whined. "This isn't the time to answer questions."

"Unless you think you can manage twenty-five miles on a broken ankle and a bullet hole in your thigh, now's the only time you have," Cord said coldly. "Tell me what I want to know or we'll leave you here."

"You're inhuman," Gretchen said to Cord. "We can't leave this poor soul here. That wouldn't be Christian."

"I'll say a few words over his body when we bury him," Cord said. "That should set things right."

The man's eyes traveled from Cord to Gretchen and back to Cord again. "My name's Ben Sykes," he finally said. "Some folks call me Beady Ben because my eyes is set close together. Others call me Yella Ben, not cuz I'm a coward, mind, but my liver ain't first rate and I get the jaundice now and then." He looked questioningly at Gretchen as if the tale of a bad liver piled on top of a broken ankle might be enough to sway her.

"How do you know who I am?" Cord asked.

"I got a small reputation for being a hard man," Ben said, apparently straying from the point. "Nothing like the way you're known, Diamondback, but when I walk into a saloon, I get my space at the bar. About a week ago, a man hired me and three other local hardcases. Said there was two hundred dollars apiece for a few day's work."

"What did this fellow look like?"

Ben winced. "You got some whiskey for this pain?"

"What did he look like?" Cord repeated.

Ben stared at Cord for a few minutes, then obviously made a decision to cooperate. "His face ain't all that imposing," he said. "His nose is so skinny, it's hardly there. Not much of a chin to speak of and his lips and mouth are thick and greasy like he's been chewing on fat. But it's the eyes that get you. I never seen eyes that mean on a man before."

"What is his name?" Cord asked, not bothering to hide the sharpening edge in his voice.

"Never did tell us his name," Ben said. "Had the initials G.B. cut into his saddle horn though."

"Did he hire you to shoot at the miners?" Cord asked.

Ben chuckled in spite of his obvious pain. "He don't need no help in long-distance shooting. Not that curly wolf. He showed us who was boss with a gun before we were two hours on the trail. You know how crows are always smart enough to stay just outside of rifle range? Well, these two crows were soaring in an updraft about two hundred yards downwind from us and maybe a hundred yards in the air. Old G.B. don't even stop his horse. He pulled a Winchester '73 single-shot out of its casing, put the thing to his shoulder for no more than half a second and knocked one crow right out of the sky. I swear he had a new load in the chamber before the bullet hit the bird. The other crow started cawing and headed straight away from us, but G.B. picked him off too."

"If you weren't supposed to help in sniping at the miners, what were you going to do?"

"The plan was to follow you around," Ben said. "You know, make some trouble after you left. If you talked to a rancher, we wuz to shoot up that ranch house. When you met with the farmers, we wuz going to burn a few barns."

"So that's why you were interested in my movements," Cord said. "Why were you running away?"

"This ride ain't coming cheap," Ben complained. "One of the men with us was Ike Dugan. Ike's thirstier for money than most. He got talking about how G.B. must have more than two hundred apiece in his saddlebags. Ike was afraid of him, just like me and Tom, but he got the notion that maybe we didn't have to raid no farms to make our money, and maybe we could make a mite more.

" 'We can take him,' Dugan whispered to me and Tom. 'He's got a backside just like any other man.' For a little man, Dugan was tall on spunk."

"He was going to shoot his partner in the back?" Gretchen asked. "You call that spunk?"

"I thought he was crazy," Ben said. "So did Tom. That G.B. handled guns like they was connected to his body. We told Dugan he was on his own."

"That was heroic of you," Cord said.

Ben shook his head. "That was common sense. One morning when G.B. was squatting on his haunches, shaving, Dugan made his move. He snuck up behind G.B. until he was maybe fifteen feet away. No way the man could have known Dugan was there. Dugan pulled his pistol and took careful aim. He knew he'd only get one chance."

"This is so cowardly," Gretchen said.

"Seemed wise to me," Ben said. "But G.B. pulled a trick I ain't never seen done before. His holster operates on a swivel. He swung his gun toward Dugan, upside down in the holster, and plugged him twice. Dugan sprouted two more belly buttons in a hurry. The amazing thing is that G.B. never turned around. He shot Dugan with his back turned." Ben shook his head again. "Maybe he saw Dugan's reflection in his shaving mirror."

"I've never heard of shooting like that," Gretchen declared.

"I have," Cord said thoughtfully.

"The man's not human!" Ben said. "Next he asks if me and Tom want to have a go. He still ain't turned around. 'It's two-to-one,' he says. I just stood there. Tom dropped his gun belt."

"That doesn't explain the hole in your thigh," Cord said.

"When I seen what happened to Ike, I figured I'd get out of there that night," Ben said. Now that he had been forced to tell his story, he seemed anxious to give all the details. "I thought I'd just ease out of there when it got good and dark. About midnight I walked my horse out of camp, making sure to stay far away from his bedroll. I mounted and thought I was clear when I heard him call my name. 'Hey, Yella Ben.' His voice came floating down the trail like it was mocking me. Then my leg feels like it's been kicked by a Missouri mule. I look down and a red circle is spreading across my pants leg. I set the spurs to my horse and rode hard till he run out of oats."

Ben looked anxiously at Gretchen and Cord. "There was no moon last night! That man put a bullet in me from two hundred yards or more when it was pitch black!"

"What happened to the third man?" Cord asked.

"Tom? As far as I know he's still with G.B. He's stuck. He can't run away and he sure as hell can't shoot it out."

"Answer one last question and we can get started down into the valley," Cord said. "Where was your camp?"

Ben's face took on a more frightened look. "I can't tell you that. He'll find out somehow. I'm laid up and he'll come after me. Hell, he don't need to get too close."

"We'll leave you here," Cord threatened.

"Go ahead. You're giving me a choice of dying now, or dying a few days from now. Maybe somebody else will come down the trail."

"Suit yourself." Cord walked to the clump of juniper bushes and brought their horses out into the open.

"We can't leave him here," Gretchen said. "We're sentencing him to death."

"He sentenced himself."

"This man needs our help," Gretchen insisted. "I'm staying."

"Okay," Cord said. He mounted his Appaloosa and tied Gretchen's horse behind. "I'm taking both horses. You'll have to drag him down the mountain for twenty-five miles."

Gretchen glared at Cord. "I don't know how I

could have thought that you would make a fair judge. You're no different than the miners."

"Hey, lady, you really going to let him leave me here?" Ben asked.

Cord nudged his horse out at a walk. Gretchen watched helplessly, twisting her head to look back at Ben, now sitting upright, searching for a stick to support his leg.

"You win, Diamondback," Ben said. "We both know I wouldn't last the night up here, even if she stays."

Cord reined the horses, sitting upright in the saddle without turning around. "I'm listening."

"We busted into a line cabin up in the hills that belongs to one of the ranches. Old G.B. seemed to know about the place. Said he'd been up here three or four times in the past two months. Always had to go back to Denver, though, to wet his whistle or to see the elephant or something."

"That explains why the snipings at the miners' camp were sporadic."

"I know the place," Gretchen said. "There's only one line camp around here. Diamondback, this is proof of how far the ranchers are prepared to go. That camp belongs to Lafe Parsons!"

Diamondback didn't say anything. He'd been around enough to know real proof was as elusive as true love. Still, it did mean something. It meant there'd be a lot more trouble now.

Up on a hill overlooking the wagon-rut road, a man with the initials G.B. carved into his saddle horn carefully removed his Winchester '73 from its suede leather scabbard. He calibrated the sights for four hundred yards, the distance he estimated between him and the small party of three people partially obscured by the small clump of juniper bushes. He wet a finger, held it to the breeze and recalibrated the sights for drift. He took a .44-caliber slug from his navy Colt and placed it in the chamber of the Winchester. The Colt and the Winchester took the same caliber and he always traded cartridges before an important shot. It meant his guns were wed to one another and to him. He never missed when he completed this ritual. Never.

The gunman watched as a man and woman laboriously lifted a second man to a horse. He sat down in the tall grass, knees raised and legs spread wide. The man put the iron-shod butt of the Winchester next to his shoulder and braced his elbows by supporting them on the insides of his spread knees. He watched a leaf fall to be sure the wind hadn't shifted direction. He sighted the rifle carefully until a head rested on the tip of the front sight like a pie on a window ledge. He took a deep breath, exhaled slowly and gently squeezed the trigger. So gently that even he wouldn't know the precise split second when the butt kicked against his shoulder. The gun exploded. He turned quickly toward his horse without bothering to view the result. No need. He knew.

15

The bullet tumbled over and over in flight like an acrobat doing endless somersaults. A tiny explosion slapped against Cord's ear like the sound of a hammer pounding down a nail. He ducked involuntarily even though he knew that by the time he heard the shot the bullet had reached its destination.

The lead crashed into Yella Ben's temple, tunneled through his brain and burst out the top of his skull. Cord saw Ben's head erupt like a small Vesuvius of bone, blood and hair. Ben's mouth opened and curled up in a death-mask grin. His body slipped off Gretchen's horse, his open skull leaking red fertilizer to the forest ferns.

Gretchen slipped out of her saddle, beating Cord in dismounting. She flattened to the ground as Cord crawled toward her, pushing away the weeds and ferns that slapped against his face. They inched on their bellies through rust-colored pine needles until they were behind the cover of a rotting log.

"What happened?" Gretchen screamed.

"Be still." Cord looked upward in the direction of the sound of the rifle shot and saw only stump pine and boulders above him.

"Why don't you shoot back?"

Cord rose slowly. "I think he's gone. We can go now."

"Get down!" Gretchen almost begged. "How can you be sure he's not still waiting?"

"Because we're not dead," Cord said. "He had open shots at all three of us but only went after Ben. Whoever this sniper is, he's very selective about his targets."

Cord stood in the open for a moment to assure Gretchen they were safe, then helped her to her horse.

"Wait," she said. "We can't leave that poor man's body here. It isn't Christian."

"Say a few words over him if you like," Cord said. "I'll wait. Just keep the sermon short."

"He's got to be buried," she insisted. "The varmints will get him. You dig a grave. I'll make a cross."

"What if the sniper comes back while we're conducting services?" Cord asked. "Do you think he'll join in the hymns?"

"I'm not going to leave a dead man lying on the ground," Gretchen said. She had a determined look in her eyes.

Cord saw that she meant it. He needed Gretchen to establish contact with the other farmers. He lifted Ben's body, staggering slightly under the weight, and hoisted it to a tree branch six feet from the ground. "That should be high enough to keep scavengers from getting to it," Cord said. "We can send someone back for the body in the morning."

"This looks like one of those well-tended Amish farms in Pennsylvania," Cord said as they approached Gretchen's place. "Do you work it yourself?"

"I have two daughters who are old enough to help," Gretchen said. "They're with a neighbor tonight."

"That's a good place to leave them when you're off dynamiting."

"You think I was wrong?" The mercurial spark in her eyes flashed brightly. "After you saw what those miners were like? I'm beginning to think we made a mistake in listening to Mr. Mellard when he offered us your services."

"Jay Mellard persuaded you to take me?" Cord didn't bother to hide his surprise. "I thought you and Lafe Parsons specifically asked me to arbitrate this dispute."

"How could I do that?" Gretchen asked, her blue eyes staring at Cord as if he were crazy. "I never heard of you before Mellard mentioned your name. He said we had to get our problems settled if we wanted a rail line in here. The only reason I agreed to *Cord Diamondback*"—he noticed the sarcastic emphasis when she said his name—"was because I saw that Lafe Parsons wasn't too keen on using an outsider. If he didn't like the idea, it was good enough for me. Why, is something wrong?"

"No," Cord said, thinking back to how Mellard had stretched the truth by telling him both sides had requested his services. Perhaps Mellard had just been buttering him up. The young man had the markings of a typical business executive.

"Will you stay for dinner?" Gretchen asked, as their horses trotted through the gate. "All I'm offering is potluck."

"I'm staying," Cord said. "I've heard of Amish potluck."

"Then pump some water and get wood for the stove. Earn your supper!"

Cord primed the pump with a little brackish water and pulled hard for a good ten minutes before a thin trickle of cool water drizzled to the bottom of the wooden pail. This valley was short of water. He broke up some kindling for Gretchen's stove and picked out four pine logs, well dried and seasoned for a good-sized fire in the stone fireplace. The coming night would bring on a chill. He watched Gretchen busy herself in the kitchen, wisps of her blond hair unraveling from her braided bun. Her light skin had the delicate look of glazed porcelain and her light blue eyes picked up the glow of the stove. Cord could not imagine that this was the same woman who had earlier blown a dam and defied the miners.

She served him a dinner of fried chicken, pickled beets and mashed potatoes with chicken gravy. Later they sat near the warmth of the hearth, not talking much, eating peach preserves and drinking strong coffee. Cord occasionally added new logs to the blaze. He felt a pang of regret, knowing he could never have a home life like this. Wife, family, home were not for Cord Diamondback. The possibility of a normal life had been killed along with Senator Fallows in San Francisco. The scars on his back ran deep, twisting his life into a strange shape.

"Your face looked grim for a moment," Gretchen said.

He glanced up at her. She had quickly understood his mood, the sign of a sympathetic person.

"Why don't you marry again, Gretchen?" Cord asked. "You must have the opportunity."

She laughed. "There's such a woman shortage out here I get a proposal a month. But I'm tired of burying husbands. My daughters and I could manage the farm very well . . . if we had enough water."

He smiled at her. He thought her delicate skin blushed.

"You mustn't stay in the house tonight," she said. "People would talk with my daughters not here. The barn isn't heated, but outside of that not too uncomfortable. I'll bring you extra blankets against the chill."

"At least I'll have the accommodations to myself," Cord said.

"Oh no you won't," Gretchen said, laughing. She stood up to get the blankets. "I'll meet you in the barn in a few minutes."

"Let's settle this up front," Cord said to the three Guernsey cows and weary plow horse in the barn. "There'll be no snoring. Anyone doesn't like it, speak up now."

The animals eyed him suspiciously. They were neatly tended with fresh straw on the floors of their stalls. Cord heard wings fluttering near the roof and thought it might be a barn owl. A wooden ladder led to the loft used for hay storage. He climbed to the loft, not believing the farm animals would abide by his orders.

"If you snuggle into the hay with these, you should be warm enough," Gretchen said when she brought the blankets. She had changed into a loose-fitting red robe that barely suggested the definition of her breasts and buttocks. Her gray-blond bun was unpinned, sending locks of hair splashing against the dark red cloth of the robe. "I could find a nightshirt for you to wear," she added. Cord thought she seemed reluctant to leave. "I know it can be uncomfortable sleeping in your clothes."

"Thanks anyway," he said, shaking his head. He didn't like the idea of wearing one of her dead husband's garments.

"You'll have to do without light," she said. "There's too much danger of fire with the kerosene lamp. These barns go up in minutes."

"I'll manage."

She went to the head of the ladder and hesitated. "Did I thank you for saving my life this morning?"

"Yes, you did, but I don't think the miners wanted to kill you."

"I'm grateful. I want you to know that." She came over to where Cord sat on the blankets, bent over and kissed him on the cheek. Her mouth lingered against his face. She smelled sweet, like summer honeysuckle. "Thank you," she whispered, then pulled away.

Cord almost pulled her back to him. He felt himself drawn to her courage. It wouldn't take much persuasion to have her share his rustic little bed. But he'd be trading on her loneliness rather than her affection. He didn't want that. Besides, to a woman like Gretchen, sex meant a long-term commitment. And Cord Diamondback was in no position to make those kinds of commitments.

"Leave all the blankets," he said.

Cord smelled something charred and burning, like bacon that had been left too long in the pan. He opened his eyes. A smoky haze drifted through the barn loft. He glanced down to the first floor of the barn. Thick smoke filled the room, clouding his view. The plow horse kicked the side of his stall and whinnied.

Fire!

Cord remembered what Gretchen had told him about these barns going up in minutes. He raced for the ladder leading down from the loft. Heat poured into the bottom of his bare feet. He stopped at the head of the ladder, putting his hand on the top rung, then quickly withdrawing it. He couldn't get out that way. Bright yellow-and-orange flames, like a fireworks display come down to ground level, eagerly devouring the barn door.

16

Cord raced to the loft window. Below, two men, working too diligently to notice him, cut open hay bales and piled the hay against the barn walls.

"Spread it loose, Buddy," one of the men directed. "The more air gets at it, the faster she goes." He appeared to be in his midfifties, with a head of curly hair, now receding rapidly, and close-together eyes.

"She's a bonfire for sure, Nick," said his young companion, a lad no more than seventeen. The boy was husky with a full face, still showing a trace of baby fat and fast-disappearing freckles.

Their outfits pegged them as ranch hands. They were wearing the leather chaps cowboys use for a day of riding through rough brush. Cord noticed that both man and boy were carrying sidearms, but neither looked like a gunman. The revolvers were worn too high for an effective draw.

Tiny flames licked under the barn walls and chewed away at the wood inside. Cinders and sparks floated to the loft and settled on the dry hay. Heat rose from the first floor, washing against Cord's face like a blast from an open oven. Downstairs, the cows cried plaintively while the plow horse smashed his hooves against the sides of his stall.

Cord wasn't worried about getting out of the barn. The drop from the window was only about ten feet. But he knew he'd be jumping into trouble. Anyone setting fire to Gretchen's farm couldn't be her friend. So far he was lucky. The cowboys were so intent on building a good bonfire they still hadn't noticed him.

He raced to his bedroll for his Smith and Wesson. He stomped out a few small fires nervously licking at the hay in the loft. The smell of burning wool, like a piece of meat turning rank, hit his nose as the flames scorched through his socks and nipped at his feet. Cord felt he had stepped into a nest of biting ants.

He rummaged through his bedroll. The revolver was gone! Gretchen must have taken it when she left last night. She had been busy around his bedroll for a few minutes when she fixed the blankets. Why? Was this a setup?

The flames eating up the barn doors had almost reached the loft, leaving behind blackened and charred wood. The heat blasted against his face like he was staring down into an open furnace. Cord's lungs worked hard trying to suck in air, but he felt he was breathing in more heat. The wooden planks smoked around the edges. Any second now and they would burst into flame.

Time to jump. Out of the frying pan—into what?

"Stop!" Gretchen screamed, flying out of the house, wearing the same robe she'd worn last night. "There's someone in the barn."

At least she's not part of a setup, Cord thought.

Nick snorted. "Hear that, Buddy? These farmers will tell any lie to save their lousy property. Lady, there ain't anything inside except a swayback horse and piss milk cows."

"You must believe me," Gretchen tugged at the older man's shirt. "There's a man inside. Save him!"

"Nick, maybe she ain't lying," the young boy, Buddy, said. He peered at the flames. Resin popped from the heat, sounding like distant pistol shots. "I said I'd help you burn the barn, but I draw the line at roasting people alive."

"I thought you had more guts," Nick said, obviously disgusted with the boy. "Don't you know you can't believe anything these clodkickers tell you?"

"I'm telling the truth." Gretchen's voice was pleading now. "There's a man inside."

The planks in the loft floor caught fire. Black smoke billowed into Cord's lungs, making it difficult for him to breathe. He suppressed a cough, not wanting to give away his presence. Better retain the surprise as long as possible. Still he waited.

"This is a warning, lady," Nick said, spreading

more hay directly under the loft window. "Next time we set fire to your house."

Cord crouched. Smoke pouring through the hole partially obscured his body, but it poured over his face, choking off his air. His eyes watered and stung. Nick bent over his rake, pushing more hay against the barn. A man's back is a good way to break a fall, Cord thought. He grabbed a wooden frame for support and heat blistered his palm. Cord kicked out into space.

"Look out!" Buddy warned.

Nick half turned, catching Cord's feet in the middle of his chest. Both men tumbled to the ground. Cord's face skidded against the yard gravel, tearing up the skin on his cheek.

"What the hell happened?" Nick said, wobbling as he tried to rise.

No point in letting him up, Cord thought. He smashed Nick across the nose with a sharp thrust of his elbow. Damn! Too high up to break anything. Nick's body fell on top of Cord's legs, preventing him from rising.

Buddy came up fast on the fallen man, holding his Colt revolver by the barrel.

"That's a good way to shoot yourself in the stomach," Cord said.

Buddy glanced down at his gun as Cord scrambled out from under Nick's legs. Still seated on the barnyard gravel, he lunged the upper half of his body toward Buddy's knees. The boy looked panicked, pulling his body back at the same time he swung the butt end of the Colt toward Cord's skull. Cord tilted his head quickly out of the way, feeling the breeze from the gun butt as it barely grazed his scalp.

Cord swung out his right hand, latched onto Buddy's boot heel and yanked upward. The boy landed on the seat of his pants next to where Nick lay sprawled, but he managed to hang on to the revolver.

Nick staggered to his feet, shaking his head to recover from Cord's elbow smash. His narrow eyes spotted the pitchfork he'd used to spread hay against the burning barn. Cord leaped toward the older man just as he reached the pitchfork.

"Stay where you are, mister." Buddy stood on the sidelines, his gun hand shaking.

Cord skidded to a stop.

Gretchen watched the action, apparently paralyzed. "I can use a hand," Cord scolded.

"You're going to get a hand with a pitchfork in it," Nick said, advancing toward Cord. "Buddy, if he moves, plug him."

Cord watched Nick approach, the pitchfork held chest high. His eyes slid briefly toward Buddy. Would the young man shoot? Nick obviously meant to gut him.

Cord stood motionless, waiting for Nick to make his first thrust. "Cool, ain't ya?" Nick said. "You'll be cooler when you're ventilated."

Cord ignored the pitchfork, concentrating on Nick's shoulders. They would tell him when Nick made his move. Nick feinted several short thrusts with the pitchfork. Cord remained stock still. Cord saw Nick's knuckles tighten on the wooden handle. He moved his shoulders back and lunged forward,

aiming the points of the fork toward Cord's gut.
Cord pivoted like a bullfighter avoiding a charging
bull. He brought his fist down on the pitchfork
handle in a flat chopping motion. The weapon
flew out of Nick's hand, landing on the gravel,
close to Gretchen.

"Pick it up," Cord told her. Gretchen nodded
and leaned down to pick up the pitchfork.

"For Christ's sake, shoot the bastard," Nick yelled
at Buddy. "Can't you see what he's doing to me?"

"We wuz burning him alive," Buddy protested,
as if explaining to his friend that Cord's action was
justified.

Cord hammered Nick across the back of the
neck with a rabbit punch that silenced him into
unconsciousness. He turned to face Buddy, who
covered him with his revolver. The boy's hands
were shaking and his face was white. Gretchen
clutched the pitchfork in both hands. She held it
helplessly, too far away from Buddy to use it.

"You planning on firing that?" Cord asked the
boy.

"Looks like I'm going to have to," Buddy said.
"You hurt my friend. Went after me too."

"I was protecting myself," Cord said. "I was in
that barn you were burning down."

"We didn't know you wuz there, I swear it."

"Is this your profession?" Cord asked. "Burning
barns?"

Buddy's face flushed, making his fading freckles
stand out strong again. "We're just trying to get
rid of folks that don't belong on range land. I

didn't know it would go this far. I mean, who expects farmers to put up a fight."

Cord noticed the revolver barrel drooping. He thought he could probably rush Buddy and take the gun away from him, but he wanted to give the boy a chance to make his own decision. So far, that way was working, for both of them.

Gretchen dropped her pitchfork. "My animals," she cried. She rushed toward the burning barn.

Cord caught up to her in two strides. He held her back, lifting her body off the ground. "It's too late for them," he said.

"I've got to try," she said.

Buddy holstered his gun. "Lady," he said. "That barn is burning all to hell."

"I'm not asking you to do anything but let me go," Gretchen said.

Cord looked at her, knowing she meant what she said. "You stay there," he said. He turned toward Buddy. "How about giving me a hand?"

"What do you have in mind?"

"Get your horse."

Buddy ran to his horse, a skittish mustang tied to a tree about fifty feet from the barn. The mustang's eyes went wide with terror as Buddy tried to bring him closer to the blaze. His hooves pawed at the gravel and he swung his head from side to side. Buddy twisted the mustang's bit and forced him closer to the barn.

"How good a cowpuncher are you, Buddy?" Cord asked.

"I'm good enough, but I don't know a damn thing about putting out fires."

"See that bale hook on the side wall near the loft window? Can you get your rope around that?"

Buddy squinted and looked at the hook used to pulley hay bales into the loft. "Sure, I can reach that, but the fire has already reached that spot. My rope will be burned to cinders in a few minutes."

"Then we'll have to move fast."

Buddy untied his lariat from his saddle pommel and made a few practice circles. "Hurry," Gretchen pleaded.

Buddy cast the rope toward the hook. His first attempt failed and the rope fell to the ground. Buddy rewound it fast, but Cord could see that the rope had been slightly charred from the split second spent in contact with the blazing barn.

Buddy's lasso lashed around the hook on his third try. He seemed to know what to do next without Cord's instructions. He wound his end of the lariat around the saddle horn and hit his mustang once on the rump. The horse bolted straight away from the fire, coming to a skidding stop when the rope played out. Buddy dug his spurs hard into the mustang's sweaty flank. The horse, nostrils flaring, reared and plunged forward again. He pawed at the ground, his hooves scattering gravel across the barnyard. Cord saw the rope close to the hook burst into flame. It would snap any second now. Buddy whipped the mustang's rump with his open hand.

There was a creak like the sound of an old casket opening.

"Get back!" Cord warned Gretchen as the front

barn wall came crashing down, sending a shower of sparks and cinders flying into the air like a miniature Fourth of July celebration.

The inside of the barn looked like the interior of a fully stoked wood stove. "It's too late," Gretchen cried.

Cord tented the jacket over his head and rushed into the burning barn. Waves of cruel heat tugged at his skin like prickly fingers.

His skin puckered as the heat infested his clothes. He felt as if he was shriveling, his very bones drying out. The cows were still standing, but their coats were now smoking from the heat and flying cinders. They lifted their heads and cried at Cord. He fumbled with the ropes that lashed them to their stalls. One by one he pushed their heads against his stomach and moved them backward out of their stalls. He grabbed their lead ropes and led them toward the wall that Buddy had knocked down. Flames sprouted around their hooves. When the cows hesitated before the escape hole, Cord slapped their rumps with a burning timber. They trotted to safety.

The plow horse reared and snorted in total panic. He wouldn't allow Cord in his stall, lashing out with his hooves as if trying to stamp out the fire. Cord knew the horse wouldn't leave by himself as the cows had done.

"It's okay, boy," Cord soothed as he moved cautiously toward the horse.

"You'd better come out while you still can," Buddy called from outside the barn. "She's going any second now."

A heavy roof timber crashed to the floor less than six feet from Cord. He removed his jacket from his head and wrapped it around the horse's eyes from outside his stall. He untied the horse, grabbed the bridle and tried leading him out of the barn. Even blinded, the animal didn't want to go anywhere. Without his jacket, Cord felt his head was being incinerated. He wrapped both his arms around the horse's neck, jerked the nag's head down and bit hard on his ear. His teeth crunched down on horse hair and horse flesh. The horse whinnied, shook his head in an effort to get rid of the pain and finally came quietly. Cord spit out horse hair. Roof timbers fell all around him. Cord led the horse, picking his way through the flames, toward the door. As they cleared the barn the roof and remaining walls collapsed, sending fresh sparks thirty feet into the air.

Gretchen ran to her plow horse and hugged the animal around his neck. Cord patted his clothing, tamping out lighted cinders.

Buddy led the cows past Gretchen's front yard to a small pasture. Cord caught up with him. "You made up for some of what happened earlier."

Buddy flushed, his disappearing freckles standing out sharp and clear again. "Nick told me we wouldn't hurt anyone. We wuz just trying to get the damn farmers out of this valley."

"Burning property isn't hurting anyone?" Gretchen asked as she let the horse into the same pasture. "Trying to force people off their land isn't doing harm?"

"Who gave you the orders?" Cord asked the boy.

"Lafe Parsons!" Gretchen said, answering for Buddy. "These scum are both his men." She glared at the boy. "Don't you deny it."

"We work for Mr. Parsons," Buddy admitted, "but I don't think he knew. This was Nick's idea. He said we wuz to give Mr. Parsons a surprise."

All three looked over at Nick, who just now was beginning to stir on the ground. His face had the groggy look of a fighter who'd been put down for the count. He appeared in no shape to admit or deny anything.

"Don't you believe him," Gretchen told Cord. "Lafe Parsons is a monster. Where do you think Nick got his orders?"

Cord ignored her.

She looked at him for agreement. "The truth is clear," she went on. "The farmers have never resorted to this kind of violence."

"What about the time you hayseeds stampeded our herd?" Buddy asked. "I knew a couple of good men that broke limbs before we had them steers turned and quieted."

"What about it, Gretchen?" Cord demanded. "Did the farmers stampede Parsons' cattle?"

Her face reddened. "They were trampling our crops," she said. "We taught Parsons not to let his cattle stray."

"You're all filled with righteous indignation," Cord said. "This reminds me of a case I had where three sons were fighting over their father's estate. Each of the sons felt he was entitled to everything.

Not one of them was willing to give up an inch of land." Cord shook his head. "First time I was ever fired three times. The boys didn't want me when they learned I intended to be fair."

"Who got the land?" Buddy asked.

"The state," Cord said. "The place was sold for back taxes. The boys were so intent on being right, they wound up with nothing."

"If right isn't important, than what brings you here?" Gretchen asked. "What do you get out of it?"

Cord barely shrugged. "Money."

Buddy nodded. "That's a good reason."

"But it doesn't speak much for your integrity," Gretchen said.

"Sure it does. Being fair is just good business sense. That's the way I get more judging jobs. Referrals." Cord sighed. "It's time I visited Lafe Parsons and got his righteous viewpoint."

"I'll go with you," Gretchen said firmly. "I know you'll get nothing but lies from Lafe Parsons. I want to be there to tell my side."

Cord looked at her with amusement. "Suit yourself, but it seems to me you've told your side several times."

"I ain't sure Nick will go," Buddy offered. The groggy cowboy was just now beginning to struggle to his feet. He sent angry glances toward Cord.

"Nick doesn't have a choice," Cord said coldly.

"I'll come," Nick said. "Hell, you couldn't keep me from riding along. When Lafe Parsons finds out what you done to two of his best hands, you'll be walking around with the Lazy P brand on your ass."

Branded! Cord thought about the brand that was already scarred across his back. He remembered the pain and the torn flesh that hung down his body in folds. Nick didn't know it, but Cord Diamondback already knew what it was to be branded.

17

"Can you keep your lips pressed closely together?" Cord asked Gretchen as they approached Lafe Parsons' ranch.

"Of course. Why?"

"I want you to practice that feat while I'm talking to Parsons. And I mean very closely together."

"Women should be seen and not heard, is that it?"

Cord's foursome trotted past an open range roundup. Circles of riders drove steers toward a holding pen. A few tame decoys quieted the herd. Cowboys cut out the cows with unbranded calves so the youngsters could be roped and pulled toward the branding irons.

"There's Mr. Parsons," Buddy said, pointing to a tall middle-aged man holding a branding iron. The man was so intent on his work he apparently ignored the approach of Cord and Gretchen riding up with two of his cowboys.

Cord trotted right to the edge of the branding fire before bringing the foursome to a halt. He stayed in his saddle, honoring the western tradition of not dismounting on a man's property until asked.

"I brung 'em to you, Mr. Parsons," Nick cried out when they stopped. "I'm dropping that meddling Denver judge right in your lap. I brung the Kreitner woman too. I gotta tell you, Buddy didn't help worth a damn. He turned tail."

Parsons had the florid face of a beefeater with a chipped and rough-hewn look that resembled an unfinished carving. A small paunch had pushed his belt buckle below his waist. He inspected the foursome more closely, just now seeing Nick's hands were tied in front of him. "What the hell is this, Nick?" he asked. "I see Buddy and it's not his tail I'm looking at." His gaze shifted to Cord Diamondback. "You leading this train?"

"I'm bringing back your barn burners," Cord said. "I'm anxious to see the kind of welcome you give them."

Parsons appeared puzzled. "Is Nick right? Are you this Diamondback fella that Mellard hired in Denver?"

"Yes," Gretchen said. "And your men almost burned him alive, along with my barn."

Parsons' eyes took on an edge of dislike as they fastened on Gretchen. "He don't look toasted to me." He held the hot branding iron in front of him as if protecting himself. "When did your barn get burned?"

"This morning," Gretchen said, pushing her horse

forward. "Your men burned it to the ground, just as you ordered."

"I never told these boys to burn any barns, yours or anyone else's." He looked at the young boy and shook his head. "I'd believe any mean thing of Nick, but I thought better of you, Buddy."

"Nick said you wanted it done," Buddy said, obviously miserable. "He said you'd probably give us a bonus when you heard about it."

"See!" Gretchen said to Cord. "He ordered the burning." She moved her horse closer to Parsons until the branding iron was almost touching his foreleg. "You know you did."

Parsons glared at Nick, ignoring Gretchen. "You two were supposed to be rounding stray calves for branding. What the hell were you doing making mischief at the Kreitner farm?"

Nick's face became sullen. "You told me and anyone else who would listen that you wanted her off the range. I even heard you say it would be worth a lot to you. I thought if she had no barn, she couldn't keep livestock. Without livestock, she got no farm."

Parsons inspected Cord carefully to see what his reaction was. "I heard you're a fair man, Diamondback. I swear I had nothing to do with this. I want her off the range, that's true. But I don't burn people's property. Don't judge me because I have fools working for me."

"You're a liar," Gretchen said quietly. The softness carried conviction.

Lafe Parsons' iron-gray eyes drilled into her. "You keep name calling and them skirts ain't going to give you much more protection. I don't lie to you or anyone else."

Cord thought that Parsons' words had the ring of truth. He seemed like a forthright man, but maybe he was just a convincing liar. Cord admitted to himself he was puzzled. Each of the parties to the dispute—Charley, Gretchen, Lafe Parsons— seemed headstrong and stubborn. No room in their heads for any view other than their own. But none of them seemed capable of cold-blooded murder. Gretchen had used violence when she dynamited the miners' dam, but even that was an act against property, not designed to hurt anyone. So who hired Snake Eyes and why? "Gretchen said your men kept her away from water at a time when the ponds were full," Cord told Parsons.

"She's got that part right," Parsons said, staring a challenge at Gretchen. "We had water all right, but not enough to let it get pissed away dousing scrawny vegetables." He finally put down the branding iron and wiped the back of his forehead with one of his huge hands. "You gotta understand what the stakes are here, Diamondback. The day of the longhorn is finished. They take ten years to mature and when they're butchered, the meat is tougher than the hide. I'm bringing in Herefords for cross-breeding. When I finish, I'll have tender beef the folks in the East will pay top dollar for. If Mellard brings in that railhead, I can load 'em here without losing weight driving them to market."

"So let's hear your idea of a fair split," Cord said, testing him.

"Let 'em find another valley." Parsons waved

his hands toward the west as if there were an endless string of sheltered valleys. "And let those
damn miners find another mountain. I was here
first. And I'm building something that's going to
last for a long, long time."

"So are the farmers," Cord reminded him. "And
the miners are claiming squatter's rights on the
water. I'm surprised a tough cattleman like you
hasn't tried to force them off."

Parsons made a face as if he'd swallowed bitter-
root. "I figured their veins would be played out by
now and they'd be gone to new diggings. When
Mellard came to me, I said I'd listen, but if you
don't come up with some answers, I'm planning to
send my men in on 'em after roundup."

"Somebody's after them already. A sniper's up
the rocks above their camp."

"Why tell me?" Parsons said. He pointed at
Gretchen. "She's got just as much cause."

"I don't think it was Gretchen," Cord said. "Her
methods are more explosive." .

"I agreed to let an outsider settle this mess
because I heard Diamondback was a fair judge,"
Parsons said. "Now, it seems you're favoring the
Kreitner woman. Just what were you doing in her
barn? Did those blue eyes get to you?"

"You're disgusting!" Gretchen said.

Cord ignored Parsons' gibe. "What are you planning to do about these two men?" he asked. "They
seem to expect a bonus."

Parsons grinned at Cord. "You think I'm a bad
hombre, don't you, Diamondback?" He turned
toward Nick. "I won't have barn burners working

for me." He walked to Nick's horse and untied his hands. "You're finished here, Nick. Use your matches on somebody else's range."

"That's my thanks after what I done on your behalf?" Nick whined. "What about my back pay?"

"I advanced you two months' wages, remember? We'll call her square if you get off my ranch by nightfall. Don't let me find you here tomorrow."

Nick grabbed for the rifle on his saddle. "You ain't kicking me out like I was a dog."

Cord's hand dropped to his holster, silently inviting the cowboy to draw his rifle. "Well, pull it out and start the party or move along."

Nick half lifted the carbine out of its casing, hesitated and let it drop back heavily.

"That's one I owe you, Diamondback," Parsons said. "I didn't think the sonofabitch had the backbone. I ain't holding. I got two pistolas in my saddlebags, but using a short-arm during branding is downright dangerous. I'd likely shoot my rump off." He picked up the branding iron and pointed it in the direction of the surrounding mountains. "Now, get out of here, both of you."

"Do I have to leave, Mr. Parsons?" Buddy asked. "I know I don't deserve it, but I'd like another chance."

"It's your business," Cord said, "but the boy helped me save Gretchen Kreitner's livestock. Your man Nick's the troublemaker."

"I know that," Parsons said. "I'm firing the boy because he's stupid. Tell you what, Buddy. If you come back in the spring, I'll put you on again. I just don't want to see your face for a time."

"Sure thing, Mr. Parsons." The boy's face brightened. He touched his hand to his head in an informal salute.

For one crazy second Cord thought the boy was pointing to a bloody hole in his forehead. The hole filled with blood that streamed down Buddy's face as Cord heard the deadly crack of a carbine. Buddy slid lifelessly out of his saddle.

Parsons ran over to the lad's body. "What the hell hap—" The carbine cracked again and Parsons flopped in the air. He landed near the red-hot branding irons, holding his thigh.

Gretchen dived out of her saddle and sprawled behind one of the calves that had been roped for branding. Nick dug the spurs to his horse and rode hell-for-leather. He was already about thirty yards down range. Most of the other cowpunchers had dropped to the ground, looking toward the rifles sitting hopelessly far away on their saddle ponies.

Cord slid in next to Gretchen behind the calf. He waited for the next crack of the carbine, remembering that Snake Eyes used a Winchester '73 single-shot. He heard the report and watched Nick's body tumble from his galloping horse. If Cord wasn't so busy going for his own gun, he would have admired the marksmanship.

When Cord reached his saddle, two bullets in quick succession whistled past his ear. The shots were so close together, they must have come from a repeater. Cord figured they hadn't come from Snake Eyes because the shots missed. He remembered the last of the toughs whom Snake Eyes had hired in Denver.

Cord dropped behind the calf again, his eyes searching the surrounding hills. Two riders were blatantly out in the open at the top of a gentle rise about four hundred yards away. One man was standing in his stirrups taking careful aim. That was Snake Eyes all right. There was something fearful about his arrogance. He disdained cover as if he were invulnerable to bullets.

Snake Eyes and the other man were side by side. Cord spread his legs wide and supported his elbows on the ground. He steadied the Springfield and took careful aim. The horsemen on the rise shifted slightly. If only they would stand still. Cord wasn't sure he could hit a moving target at that distance. He carefully squeezed off a round. The Springfield bucked against his shoulder and one of the riders dropped from his horse.

Cord cursed. He'd aimed for Snake Eyes and hit the other man. Two cowpunchers, apparently encouraged by Cord's shot, went charging up the rise. Snake Eyes dismounted, went to one knee and sent a 30-30 slug into the heart of the closest man. The dull thud of the bullet ripping through his body carried all the way down to Cord as the cowboy dropped in the tall grass. His companion turned tail and ran back down the rise as Snake Eyes reloaded his single-shot. Cord pumped off two more shots in Snake Eyes' direction, the bullets kicking up dirt at least five feet away from the target. Snake Eyes blasted the retreating cowboy in the nape of the neck, the slug carrying away his Adam's apple as it exited out front. He looked as if he was wearing a red handkerchief.

Cord thought he'd aim for a bigger target and trained his sights on Snake Eyes' cayuse. Put the bastard afoot and they'd eventually get him. Cord pulled the trigger and watched the horse stagger and fall. He heard Parsons cheer in the background like a spectator at one of Harvard's football games. The big beefeater's wound must not be serious.

Snake Eyes sent a quick shot toward Cord that thudded into the earth less than six inches from his covered position. Cord trained his sights on the other horse, but Snake Eyes jumped up, corralled the animal as Cord blasted two shots toward him. Snake Eyes threw himself into the saddle of his fallen companion's horse and disappeared over the rise. At least I made him move fast, Cord thought.

Cord examined Lafe Parsons, still lying on the ground holding his bloody thigh. His breathing was shallow and his face looked strained, but otherwise he seemed all right. "That wound won't kill you," Cord told the rancher. You'll be walking in a few days."

"Who was that slick-shooting bastard on top of the rise?" Parsons asked; his eyes were slightly glazed as if he were going into shock.

"A sniper has killed two miners," Cord said. "I'm sure this is the same man."

"If he's drilling both miners and cowboys, seems to me that's strong evidence that Kreitner here is behind him," Parsons said.

"You're the one who has paid killers on his payroll," Gretchen told Parsons.

"Farmers are the only group who haven't been shot at," Cord reminded Gretchen. "Parsons has a point."

Gretchen looked at Cord as if he had betrayed her. "I thought you were on my side," she said. Her eyes switched to Parsons, who was drinking in the exchange. "Well," she continued lamely. "I thought you believed me."

"I'm not on anyone's side," Cord said. "You folks hired me as a judge, remember?" He finished patching Parsons' gun wound with strips of cloth torn from Gretchen's petticoat. "That will hold you until you reach a doctor, but don't wait too long."

Parsons whistled for his men. "I'm sending a few riders after that bastard," he said. "Maybe they can catch up with him."

"Don't," Cord warned. "He can pick off your men before they even sight him. He's the best shot I ever saw. You're lucky he only got you in the thigh."

Parsons ordered his men to make him a litter. "I ain't going to enjoy being toted twenty miles back to my ranch," he said. His naturally florid face had whitened.

"Perhaps you could put up Lafe at your farm," Cord suggested to Gretchen.

"I only have room in the barn," Gretchen reminded Cord. "And I'll charge rent."

"I don't think I can afford your fees," Parsons said.

"Work it out any way you can," Cord said. "I'm headed in the other direction."

"Turning tail back to Denver?" Gretchen had a disappointed look on her face. "Things getting too hot for you, Dimondback?"

Cord ignored Gretchen and turned to Parsons. "I need the directions up to your line camp. I think the sniper may be holed up there."

"Let me give you a few men," Parsons said.

"A group of riders makes too much noise," Cord answered. "The only chance I have is getting close and surprising him. His edge is long-distance accuracy with a rifle. If I can get close enough, I can take that edge away."

Parsons shook his head pessimistically. "From what I've seen, nobody gets that close."

"I'll go with you," Gretchen said. "Maybe I can help."

Cord smiled at her. "Thanks for the offer. If I decide to dynamite the cabin, I'll send for you."

"You can't go up there alone."

"It's better than waiting down here so he can use me for target practice."

"Just because he used my cabin once, doesn't mean he'll still be there," Parsons said.

"He'll be there," Cord said. "Snake Eyes will be waiting for his payoff. And I know who's going to show up with the money."

18

Cord pushed his Appaloosa along the mountain trail leading to Parsons' line camp.

"Careful, boy," he whispered, letting the horse pick his way through the dark. Black night suited Cord's purpose. He couldn't see, but neither could he be seen.

He almost passed the cabin in the dark. No light showed from the crude, one-room shelter. No smoke floated from the chimney. He heard a horse softly pawing the ground. The place must be occupied.

Line cabins were used to provide a roof for cowboys riding the high country in search of strays. Parsons' cabin was constructed of roughly cut pine logs piled on top of one another and cemented together with dried mud. One small window had been cut into the front wall near the door.

Only a dozen feet of land around the cabin had

been cleared. Cord walked his Appaloosa to the edge of the clearing, dismounted and tied the horse to a small pine. The thin mountain air smelled clean and fresh from the surrounding pines. There was no sound except for one hoot owl and the nervous pawing of the horse that Cord still hadn't spotted. Overhead a flight of geese headed south in an uneven V formation.

Before Cord left the cover of the trees he inspected the area for signs of life. The dirty cabin window reflected the pale light of the moon, making it impossible for him to see inside. For all he knew, Snake Eyes could be sitting at that window hugging his Winchester '73.

There was nothing more to be learned without taking some chances. Cord advanced carefully, first checking his Smith and Wesson to be sure there was a bullet in every chamber. If he were being set up, he'd never hear the explosion from the gun that killed him.

Cord reached the cabin and pressed his face against the glass. The darkness inside reminded him of ocean water just after a giant squid had released its ink. He shut his eyes for a moment, accustoming them to darkness and took another squint. The contrast from total darkness to sparse light allowed him to make out shapes inside the cabin.

A bunk in one corner was empty. There were murky shadows in the room that must be solid objects. Cord squinted, trying to pierce the darkness. A square object in the center of the room must be a small table. There was a dark form draped over the table. It was the figure of a man! Cord realized that the shape must be resting on a chair with his head slumped against the table. A long narrow stick, pointed straight at the window, lay a few feet from the sleeping figure. Cord knew the man must be Snake Eyes and the stick was his Winchester.

Bursting into a room with a marksman inside, asleep or not, seemed foolhardy. Cord thought his safest play was plugging the bushwacker through the window. But then he'd never be able to prove who hired Snake Eyes.

Cord's eyes shifted to the inside of the cabin door. He didn't see anything propped against it. Entry should be relatively easy. Careless, Cord thought.

Cord approached the cabin door, checking his Smith and Wesson to make sure there was a bullet in every chamber. He memorized Snake Eyes' position, slumped over the table. He couldn't count on getting off more than one shot. Cord took a deep breath and slammed his foot against the doorjamb. Leather hit wood with a loud bang that silenced the surrounding crickets. The door cracked, but didn't open. Damn! He'd lost the element of surprise. Cord's foot lashed out again with even greater force. The door burst open with a loud thud that sounded like a falling redwood. Cord did a tuck-and-roll into the cabin and came up holding his revolver where Snake Eyes had been slumped over the table. He was still there snoring loudly. The racket hadn't stirred him!

The first item of business was the Winchester.

Cord took it from the table, then lit a candle. The sleeping figure wore a sidearm. Cord removed the gun, a British navy Colt with two, three-masted ships etched on the cylinder. Rare piece of hardware, Cord thought. Only a thousand pieces had been imported from England. He patted the sleeping man down for more weapons and found a knife strapped to his leg.

Cord still hadn't seen the sleeping man's face. Why didn't he awaken? Could he be in a drunken stupor? Where were the empty whiskey bottles? Cord grasped a fistful of the man's hair and yanked his face off the table. He felt sick as he saw the pale, yellow eyes of George Bennet, the cowardly poker player he'd met in Denver. He'd been right about the man. Cord realized that if he had followed his instincts and braced Bennet back at the Brown Palace, there'd be fewer corpses now.

Bennet groaned softly and opened his yellow eyes. They were dilated, the pupils big and flat as bull's-eyes. He blinked several times as if trying to focus on Cord. "Oh, it's you," he said weakly, and lapsed back into semiconsciousness. Cord shook him roughly, slapping Bennet's face hard several times before he was roused again.

Bennet's thick lips trembled; his razor-thin nose was covered with mucous. "I need help," he said. "I'm in bad shape."

"Don't expect help from me," Cord said.

The muscles in Bennet's face jumped involuntarily. He wiped the back of his sweaty forehead with a greasy hand. "I thought I had enough to last me," he said. "I was careful to bring enough, but now it's all gone. My last two bottles were in the saddlebags of that horse you shot." He glanced up at Cord hopefully. "Did you bring my saddlebags with you?"

Cord still had difficulty with Bennet's character shifts. Arrogant assassin one moment, sniveling coward the next. "I don't have any whiskey," Cord said. "Give me the name of your boss, and I'll let you sleep off your hangover. Tomorrow I'll bring you down to the valley."

"Whiskey!" Bennet's weak mouth creased in the shape of a sick smile. "What I need ain't whiskey. And I'll feel a damn sight worse in the morning if I don't get it. If I don't get some laudanum, I ain't going to make it."

Laudanum! Bennet was a dope eater. That was the reason for his personality shifts. Snake Eyes' courage came out of a bottle of snake oil. "How long have you been an addict?" Cord asked.

Bennet slumped over, holding his head with both hands. "A long time," he said. "I got the habit bad. Do you know anything about laudanum?"

"Enough to stay away from it," Cord said. "It's a painkiller, a mixture of opium and alcohol. Laudanum's been around for a couple of hundred years, but most good doctors won't touch it because it's so addictive."

"My body craves the stuff," Bennet admitted. "I hurt now. If I don't get laudanum soon, I'm going to hurt worse."

"I don't mind watching you suffer," Cord said, "but if you tell me who hired you, I'll get you to a doctor."

Bennet looked at Cord hopefully. "Has the doc got any laudanum?"

"How would I know?" Cord said. "I sure as hell don't have any."

Cord heard the soft shuffle of a boot scraping against the cabin's wooden floor. Before he could turn, the aristocratic voice of Anna Mellard said, "Don't make a bad bargain, George. Diamondback isn't promising you anything."

Cord began to pivot. "Stand still," Anna warned. "Right now I prefer looking at your back."

"But I miss the sight of your beautiful face," Cord said.

"Then turn slowly and feast your eyes," Anna said. "Jorge's covering you, and there's another pistol pointed at you from the window."

"I'm surprised that Parsons could make it up here so quickly with his wounded leg." Cord said. "I didn't expect him until morning."

"Sonofabitch," Parsons exclaimed. "I'm going to shoot that smart bastard right now."

Cord turned carefully, his arms out to his side. Anna Mellard posed elegantly in the doorframe. Jorge stood beside her, one of his pistols aimed at Cord's middle. He touched the brim of his sombrero and flashed his white teeth. Lafe Parsons glared in from the window. He held a Colt double-action .38 pointed uncertainly toward Cord.

George Bennet ran toward Anna. "Did you bring me anything?" he asked desperately.

"I have your medicine in my bag," Anna answered. "Careless of you to lose your supply."

"He shot my horse when I was working on

Parsons' cowboys," Bennet accused Cord. "I had to hustle to get out of there."

Anna Mellard gave Cord an admiring glance. "You outshot George? He was once the top trick-shot artist with Buffalo Bill's show. Bennet in his prime put Annie Oakley to shame. Maybe you remember his stage name? Major Giles Bravo. Given to Bennet by Bill himself. But George has a sad story, don't you, George?"

Cord remembered hearing about a sharpshooter who preceded Annie Oakley and Frank Butler with the Wild West Congress. The man's skill was legendary, but he dropped out of sight a few years ago.

"Hey, smartass," Parsons called, "how the hell did you know it was me standing behind you? After all Bennet put a hole in me too."

"It was *where* he put the hole," Cord said. "First, Bennet had his choice of targets, you or Buddy, and he took down Buddy. He still had time to reload and get off a clear, unhurried shot at you and only managed to crease your thigh. That started me thinking. Your friend, Snake Eyes, never misses."

Parsons glared at Anna. "You said that getting shot would throw suspicion off me. Looks like I got plugged for nothing."

"Your wound is less than a bee's kiss, señor," Jorge said.

"Shut up, spic," Parsons said loudly. "Or you'll get kissed by the bees in this .38."

"I suspected you anyway," Cord admitted. "I didn't buy your story about Buddy and Nick operating on their own when they burned Gretchen's barn. They weren't that enterprising. And I wondered how you knew that Bennet had once used your line cabin."

Bennet paid no attention to the conversation as he rummaged through Anna's bag, searching for the pint bottle of laudanum. When his nervous hands found the bottle, he lifted it to his greasy lips and drank deeply. He sat back with a sigh, his face changing, becoming confident, self-controlled and deadly.

"I give up my soul to this stuff," Bennet said, waving the brown bottle in a small protective arc. "Some of the shooting contests me and Annie had, we'd let fly more than a thousand rounds. My shoulder would turn to raw meat from the kick of the carbine. I couldn't shoot well from anticipating pain as I squeezed the trigger. Some quack recommended this stuff. Worked fine and steadied my nerves. Gave me a better, more peaceful feeling than booze. Pretty soon I couldn't do without it. Went on stage one night when my supply ran dry and killed an Injun. He was a no-account buck, but Cody gave me my walking papers. Don't tell me it was because of one red-ass Injun! I could outshoot Annie and that snot-nose Butler too."

"Jay discovered George in Denver," Anna Mellard said. "You remember how my son worships the heroes of the West. Of course Jay dropped him when he learned about George's filthy habits. The disillusionment of youth. I put Bennet on my payroll. He makes a perfect assassin."

"You mean deadly, but controllable," Cord said.

"I knew you'd understand." Anna Mellard smiled. "Laudanum's an expensive habit. Did you know they used to mix the opium with gold and pearls? It was a painkiller for royalty back in those days. It's still very dear and George pays me back in the only currency he has."

"I'd like to get that Buffalo bagger in my sights," Bennet said, still carrying on about Cody. The laudanum had restored his nerves. He retrieved his Winchester and British navy Colt from Cord and reloaded both weapons. "Who gets to plug him?" he asked Anna, pointing at Cord. "I'm volunteering."

Lafe Parsons had stepped around from outside the window into the cabin. A bandage was tightly wrapped around his thigh. "Give him to me," he argued. "My leg still hurts and I had to ride like hell to get up here. Somebody's going to pay for my pain."

"I take him," Jorge said. "I owe him something for Denver."

Anna Mellard awarded Cord a thin smile. "You're very much in demand. What's your preference?"

"I would prefer to stay alive," Cord said. He had to speak cautiously now because he had miscalculated. He had expected Parsons to follow him up to the line cabin. He had carefully baited the trail. But he didn't anticipate the cattleman making it up the mountain so quickly with a wounded leg. Cord had no time to set his trap. Anna Mellard was an unexpected bonus—and Jorge an extra threat.

"That's not one of the options open to you," Anna told Cord.

"Keeping me alive is in your interest too," Cord said. "You know none of these men is trustworthy."

Anna Mellard appeared amused. "A mercenary judge doesn't instill confidence either."

"I told no one that you were behind the trouble in Sheltered Valley," Cord said. "Doesn't that deserve trust?"

"You didn't know," Anna Mellard said with a trace of irritation. "I confused the issue too well."

Jorge still had his pistol trained at Cord's middle, but Parsons' Colt sagged to his side. Bennet sipped his laudanum, his eyes carelessly covering the room.

Cord laughed softly. "Confused the issue? You were transparent! That night when you visited my room in Denver, you claimed you wanted me to find Valerie's killer. I knew that wasn't your real purpose. You don't want peace in this valley."

Cord noticed Lafe Parsons bristle when he mentioned Anna's visit to his room. Apparently she made other midnight calls. That's how she was controlling the beefy cowman.

"What's he saying, Anna?" Parsons asked. "Did you go to Diamondback?"

"Oh shut up, Lafe," Anna snapped, really annoyed now. "I scratched your itch. Isn't that enough?"

"You said I'd be the biggest cattle baron in Colorado when this was finished," Parsons continued. "I thought we were going to share that."

"If you just keep doing what I tell you, the land

will be yours, Lafe," Anna said. "I've made no other promises."

"How are you going to get those cows to market?" Cord asked. "Anna wants to kill the plan for the spur line."

"That's just temporary," Lafe Parsons answered, "until we can get the farmers and miners out of here. I'll pick up their land, and *then* the line will go through."

"Anna doesn't want the line built, ever," Cord said. "She's a big stockholder in the railroad and thinks it's too risky, don't you, Anna?"

"Jay is going to bankrupt the line," Anna said. She looked over at Lafe. "The time isn't right for a spur line here."

"Rich people think too much," Jorge said.

"What Anna means is that her husband left her several million shares of Denver Pacific Railroad stock and she doesn't want to take chances with it," Cord said.

"My husband was a clerk in a law office when I met him," Anna Mellard said. "I worked in a linen shop for three years so we could invest in our first business. I worked every hour he worked. I matched him scheme for scheme. We got rich together. Then when he died, he left everything to Jay. Everything! I don't own those shares, Mr. Diamondback, just the income as long as I live. And my fool son is making certain there will be no income. Bringing a line this way would be a disaster."

She looked at Cord with a new measure of

respect. "You got quite a lot out of one midnight meeting."

"You're forgetting our first meeting," Cord told her. "Remember that night when you and Jorge burst into my room at the Brown Palace?" Jorge glared, showing he remembered. "When I said I had bad news about your employee, you knew I was referring to Valerie. She was supposed to be working for Jay. Valerie was actually in your secret employ, wasn't she?"

"You deduced all that from one chance remark?" Anna asked. "That's presumptuous."

"There was nothing presumptuous about the marks your diamond ring left on my bottom," Cord said. "They were identical to the marks on Valerie's back."

This time it was Lafe Parsons who glared at Cord.

"Jay doesn't consult me anymore," Anna Mellard admitted. "I needed someone inside to let me know what was going on. The poor girl occasionally needed to be reminded where her loyalties lay."

"Then you had her killed because you were afraid that she'd tell Jay about your scheme. You knew Valerie couldn't take pressure."

Anna Mellard's perfectly oval face dropped its mask of haughtiness and she replaced it with a look of total hate. "Diamondback, you're much too clever to trust." She fixed Parsons with a commanding stare. "Lafe, here's the chance you wanted."

Lafe cocked the hammer of his Remington. He

carefully pointed the weapon at a point on Cord's forehead. He nervously wiped his mouth with the back of his left hand as his trigger finger tightened.

"That's it, Parsons," Jorge said. "Shoot the bastard where he stands."

19

Lafe Parsons glanced unsurely toward Anna Mellard. "Five minutes ago I was anxious to throw a couple of slugs into this fast-talking bastard. He still needs killing, but why the hell should I do it? I don't trust you enough, Anna, to have you as a witness to murder. Maybe you got some more surprises for me. Let one of your hired thugs kill him."

Bennet sat quietly at the table, listening to the exchange between Parsons and Mellard. His left hand caressed the Winchester.

"I kill him for you, señora," Jorge said, taking a step toward Cord. *"Con mucho gusto."*

"Step away, Jorge," Anna ordered. "Lafe, I want to be certain you have as much at stake as I do. You kill Diamondback."

Jorge stepped back with a shrug and holstered his pistol. Cord moved closer to Parsons while he was still hesitant. He walked to within a few feet of the cattleman. "What did she promise you?"

Parsons looked at Cord, obviously not wanting to hear any more. "You're right, Anna," he said. "We've talked too much." He raised his pistol toward Cord's heart.

Cord braced his body on one leg and lashed out the other leg toward Parsons' wounded thigh. The toe of his boot crashed dead center into a dried blood spot on Parsons' bandage. Cord could see his toe making a tiny momentary crater on Parsons' thigh.

The cattleman's roar of pain sounded like the bleat of a gored longhorn. His leg crumpled under him and his beefy body fell to the floor with a thump that raised dust. His pistol arm flew up and two shots thudded harmlessly into the pine-log walls.

Jorge crossed his arms for a reverse draw of his pistols, but Cord butted into him just as the Mexican cleared leather. One of the pistols fired, drilling a hole in the floor less than a foot from Parsons' crotch.

"Get him!" Anna Mellard screamed.

Bennet's yellow eyes glistened with deadly joy. He carefully set down his bottle of laudanum as if he were handling a crystal goblet and snatched up his Winchester.

Cord dashed out the cabin door and streaked toward a clump of oleander bushes about fifteen feet from the cabin. No time to reach the Appaloosa. Glass crashed behind him. Damn! Bennet must be drawing down on him from the window. If the sharpshooter had run for the door, he'd have taken a few more precious seconds. Cord hurtled the last five feet to the cover of the shrubs. He dived headlong toward the evergreens just as Bennet's rifle exploded. Cord felt his shoulder wrench as it took the brunt of his weight when he landed.

The pain in his shoulder persisted, even grew stronger. Perhaps he had hit a rock when he rolled. He glanced down and saw the neat hole leaking blood onto his shirt.

A clatter of feet came running out the cabin door. "You didn't get him," Jorge said.

Bullets ripped through the shrubs, sending a shower of leaves falling on Cord. He took off running into the pine trees, dodging off to his left. No time to worry about gunshot wounds. He could still hear their voices in the clearing near the cabin.

"You two go after him," Bennet said. "Just flush him into the open for one second. That's all the time I need."

"We'll take the pistols," Parsons told Bennet. "You keep the Remington repeater here. You might need more than one shot."

"Never needed more than one before," Bennet said. His voice brimmed with an addict's confidence.

"Just get him!" Anna Mellard said.

Cord kept moving to his left, traveling in a semicircle about thirty-five feet from the cabin. Could Jorge track? Cord glanced back and saw a trail of blood that looked like it had been made by a punctured paint can. No tracking experience needed to follow that trail. I've got to plug up my wound somehow, he thought. He tore several leaves from the low-hanging branch of a tree and plastered them against the spot where blood oozed from his shirt. The leaves soon turned red, but a trickle of blood still moved down his arm.

Cord moved lightly, quietly, but dried leaves on the forest floor announced every step he took. The shock of the slug ripping through his flesh had passed and Cord's shoulder throbbed with a fast steady pain like a metronome gone crazy.

The first fringe of dawn touched the night sky. Morning light would make him easier to spot. The mountain air still held the night's chill, but Cord sweated from exertion.

"Be sure you know who you're shooting at," Jorge said.

Cord tried to place his location from the sound of Jorge's voice.

"Whatcha worried about?" Bennet shouted back. "I never kill anyone by accident."

Cord almost stepped on a fat red spider spinning an enormous web between two dead tree branches. He knocked the spider off his trap, scooped up the web and carefully applied it to his shoulder wound. The web felt sticky, yet silky like a gossamer gauze. His wound seemed to absorb the spider silk. Dead flies and bettles, sucked dry of their juices by the spider, still clung to strands. Cord felt queasy, but the bandage worked. His bleeding stopped.

He searched the ground for possible weapons and found a fallen branch about three feet long and one inch thick. Not much firepower against three men armed with rifles and pistols, including the man reputed to be the greatest crack shot in the history of the West.

Cord heard Parsons and Jorge crashing through the forest, coming straight toward him. He scanned the area, looking for a promising spot to ambush the pair. Not enough cover anywhere.

Cord zigzagged sharply from the point where his blood trail ended so Jorge and Parsons couldn't keep their straight line pursuit. The pain in his shoulder crept down relentlessly, like a stain spreading across water, until his entire left side ached. The left arm would be useless in a fight. Maybe it didn't matter because they had no intention of letting him get close enough to land blows.

"Looks like he's circling," Jorge called to Bennet. "Careful he don't sneak up behind you."

"No way that can happen," Bennet answered back. His voice came from a high place. Cord realized the sharpshooter had climbed to the roof of the line cabin so he'd have a clear field of fire the minute Cord popped into view.

Cord added several stones, the size of his fist, to his puny arsenal. He took off his shirt, tying the arms together. If Parsons or Jorge maneuvered close enough, they'd see the ridged scars on his back. Not that it mattered. If they got that close, he'd be dead. They could call his corpse Diamondback, or Deacon, or anything they liked.

Cord plastered himself against the far side of a pine tree. He waited, forcing himself to think like a hunter rather than the hunted. But how could

an unarmed man attack two men with pistols? If
they had separated, he might be able to catch one
of the men unaware. He heard them approach his
tree—together.

"We're wasting our time," Jorge told Parsons.
They were standing less than ten feet away. "He's
not stupid enough to try to take three men. I'll
bet he's hotfooted straight away from the cabin
headed for the valley."

"That's not the way he was moving when we
lost his trail," Parsons replied. "He's still around
here someplace. If I'm wrong, we can give him a
few hours' head start and still mount up and catch
him. He's afoot, remember?"

Jorge and Parsons advanced again, the argument apparently resolved in favor of the man paying
the bills. They were only a few feet from Cord's
tree, their pistols drawn and ready. Cord cradled
the stones he had picked up in a nest made by the
body of his shirt. He flung the shirt above his
head like a slingshot, arcing the stones in a high
semicircle behind his pursuers. The stones bounced
heavily among the pine branches and fell to earth.

"Did you hear that?" Parsons asked. "He's got-
ten behind us somehow."

"He's noisy all of a sudden," Jorge said suspiciously. "What's he doing back there, screwing a
bear?" Jorge cupped his hands. "Hey Bennet! You
see anything?"

"When I see him you'll hear my rifle," Bennet
called back.

"Well, check it out." Parsons' voice sounded

impatient. "Maybe he fell or fainted from loss of blood. Get over there before he's long gone."

"I'll bet you don't know how to run your damn ranch either," Jorge grumbled as he walked off. "Stay sharp, Parsons. That bastard is sneaky."

The pain from Cord's shoulder permeated his entire body. His lungs felt as if they couldn't take in enough air. Surely Parsons could hear him gasping for breath.

Cord had hoped that Parsons would continue advancing toward the tree so he could whack the rancher with a stick as he went past. But Parsons stood in one spot, apparently waiting for Jorge to report.

Time to roll the dice, Cord thought, Jorge will be back any minute. Cord willed down his pain, pushing it off into the distance. He stepped from behind the tree trunk and spotted Parsons faced in the direction where the stones had landed. Parsons held his Colt loosely at his side as he stared after the disappeared Jorge. Cord closed the distance between them. Some instinct caused Parsons to turn just as Cord swung the tree branch toward the cattleman's head. Parsons hurriedly raised his pistol toward Cord, at the same time shouting out, "Jorge."

Cord lowered the branch's trajectory in midswing, shattering it into kindling against Parsons' gun hand. Cord was left with a stick less than a foot long as a red welt appeared on Parsons' hand. The Colt flew out and accidentally discharged as it landed on its butt about six feet from the two men.

"Damn it, Jorge, get back here quick," Parsons cried. He made the mistake of diving for the fallen Colt rather than facing Cord.

Cord conceded Parsons a six-inch lead in the race to the revolver. When the cattleman bent to snatch up his gun, Cord dropkicked him in the face. He felt bone and cartilage give way before his foot and Parsons' nose collapsed. The contact sent fresh pain lacing through Cord's body, hitting into his left side like a sledgehammer. Parsons staggered and fell among the pine needles, his bloody nostrils plastered against his cheek, blood dribbling down across his mouth and chin.

Cord heard Jorge thrashing through the forest toward them like a bear being chased by a swarm of bees. Parsons rose to one knee, fumbling toward the Colt. Cord dived toward him, pounding the cattleman in the chest with his wounded shoulder. The shock broke the fragile scab created by the spiderweb and once again blood pumped from his wound.

Parsons lay face down, gulping in air and pine needles through a wide-open mouth. Cord pushed down hard on the back of the cattleman's skull, grinding his face, broken nose and all, into the forest floor. He rolled back toward the fallen Colt just as Jorge burst into view, both pistols drawn.

Jorge skidded to a stop about twenty feet away and threw three shots toward the rolling Cord. One of the slugs kicked up dirt and pine cones near Parsons' body. "That's right, Jorge," Cord taunted, "kill Parsons. Do my work for me." He reached the Colt and rolled over one last time.

Jorge hesitated for one fatal second as Cord steadied his body and pumped two shots at the Mexican. The first bullet whistled past his head, but the second caught Jorge in the side, spinning him in a complete three-hundred-and-sixty-degree circle. He dropped his guns and clutched at his side, his black eyes looking blankly at Cord as if a terrible mistake had been made. Cord's third slug slammed through the Mexican's neck, turning his Adam's apple into apple sauce. He blinked rapidly as bits of his own flesh flew into his eyes. Jorge opened his mouth to say something, but Cord heard only the rush of escaping air. The Mexican poised for an instant, then collapsed all at once.

Parsons lifted his head from the dirt. "Don't kill me," he begged. His broken nose gave his voice a nasal sound as if he had a strong head cold. "Anna Mellard was behind this. She promised me a ranch ten times the size of the one I have now."

"What's going on down there?" Bennet asked. "You fired more lead than they did at Bull Run. Did you get him?"

"Tell him I'm dead," Cord commanded Parsons. Cord had weapons now, but they were short-range pistols against a rifle held by a premier sharpshooter. He needed some edge. He'd already tried surprise the last time.

"He's plugged all right," Parsons called to Bennet, his voice quivering. "Jorge put two slugs in his gut."

"That right, Mex?" Bennet asked. "Did you let the air out of Diamondback?"

The flies had already begun to settle on the raw

open wound that had been Jorge's neck. They preened madly, nibbling and sucking deep in ooze. Jorge was in no position to respond.

"It's not nice to fib, Parsons." Bennet snickered. "I'll bet Diamondback has your own gun pointed at your thick skull. Am I right? Huh?"

Parsons didn't respond. He looked helplessly up at Cord.

"That's what I thought. Well now, this changes things a bit. Anna, let's talk a new deal. Hey Anna, you still in the cabin? How you gonna get out and back to the comfort of Denver? I want a fifty-thousand-dollar bonus for getting you out of this mess. Parsons, you don't have to give me anything, because I figure Diamondback is going to blow your head off."

"Bennet's out of control," Parsons said to Diamondback. His face took on a conspiratorial look. "Get rid of him and the fifty-thousand-dollar bonus is yours. I know Anna will go along."

"You can't fix both sides in an election," Cord told Parsons. He raised his pistol as Parsons cringed. If I kill him now, Cord thought, that's one less problem to worry about. He looks finished, but why take the small risk of leaving him here alive?

"Don't kill me," Parsons begged. "I'll sign over half my ranch."

"You might make trading material," Cord said. He brought his gun butt down hard on Parsons' skull, listening with satisfaction to the dull thud as it landed. Parsons' eyes glazed. His beefy face became a sickly shade of pink as he slumped to the ground.

Cord advanced toward the same stand of oleander bushes that had masked his escape from the
cabin. He crawled on his stomach, moving slowly
so he wouldn't flush out any animals and alert
Bennet. He pictured Bennet sitting on the cabin
roof, searching the area for any sign of movement.
He'd be icy calm, his nerves braced by the
laudanum. Cord knew he had one tiny advantage
against the sharpshooter: Bennet didn't know where
he was. Maybe he could get close enough for a
shot before Bennet saw him. Hell, he had to get
the first shot.

Cord inched along on his belly, keeping his
revolver in front of him, until he felt safe under
the cover of the bushes. The clearing in front of
the cabin prevented him from moving closer. A
pistol shot at this range would be risky, but it was
the best chance he had. One free squeeze of the
trigger before the man had a chance to retaliate.
Cord raised his head slowly, bringing the revolver
barrel in line with the roof. He carefully moved a
branch to sight the gun. Nothing moved on the
roof. Snake Eyes was gone.

20

"Bennet? Are you listening?" Anna Mellard's voice came from inside the cabin. Cord thought it sounded desperate and strained. "Bennet, I'll go along with your proposition. Fifty thousand dollars is yours if you kill Diamondback. I'll throw in a bonus. All the laudanum you need. Do it, Bennet."

A light breeze rustling through the pines was the only sound in the forest. No sign of the sharpshooter. Cord hoped he would answer Anna, but no such luck.

"Hey, Anna, you offered me five thousand dollars to find Valerie's killer," Cord called to the cabin. "Well, I've found him. Looks like you're going to have to pay out no matter who comes out on top."

"Don't listen to him, Bennet," Anna called. "I offered him that money so he'd come to me first if he found out who you were. I was trying to protect you."

"You were trying to protect yourself," Cord said.

Bennet kept silent. Where the hell could he be? He killed from ambush, so Cord knew that he would be off in a blind somewhere, waiting for him to break from cover.

Cord thought about trying for his Appaloosa. Risky business because Bennet had probably staked out the animal. That might work to Cord's advantage. The horse could be the key.

Cord crawled toward the place where he had tethered the Appaloosa. He heard the soft pounding of hooves against the forest floor. The pounding grew louder and he could feel the ground shake as a horse and rider galloped within a few feet of his covered position. He raised his head to see Anna Mellard storm past astride his Appaloosa. Her haughty face was strained, terror filled her ice-blue eyes as she whipped the animal's rump with short frenzied strokes. Her pace was too fast for the steep downhill grade, but while the Appaloosa skidded and slid, she clutched the rein with one hand and slashed at his rump with the other.

I could shoot her for a horse thief, Cord thought, half amused. But gunfire would give away his position to Bennet and the marksman had enough of an advantage. Anna Mellard would have to wait until later. Bennet came first.

Cord scanned the horizon knowing that Bennet liked to perch up high. He saw an outcropping of rocks halfway up a hill about twenty feet from the cabin. The rocks formed a three-sided enclosure

rising about five feet above the ground. The place
was a natural one-man fortress with only one attack approach possible—straight forward into the
barrel of Bennet's Winchester.

Cord crept toward the rock formation. His left
side was almost deadened now and that was a
blessing. What to do when he got there? He knew
Bennet had to be there, but there was no way to
attack him. Cord crawled over a pine cone. He
noticed that the forest ground was covered with
freshly fallen cones bursting with pine oil. He
advanced to within fifteen feet of the rock formation
and settled behind the thick trunk of a huge pine.
Two big boulders provided a back rest. His position was just as impregnable as Bennet's.

Cord gathered up several dozen pine cones. He
pushed the pine needles that carpeted the forest
floor into small mounds and touched the mounds
with a lighted match. The needles quickly ignited,
burning with an earnest red flame. He took off his
wide leather pants belt and wrapped it tightly
around his right hand, making sure the leather
overlapped. After finding a foot-long stick, Cord
thrust his supply of cones, one-by-one, into the
small blaze. As the cones ignited, Cord scooped
them out of the fire with the stick. He grasped the
flaming cones with his leather-encased hand and
sent them soaring like rockets toward the rock
formation. The leather provided only partial protection and Cord's palm grew hotter with each
cone he touched. The singed leather smelled much
the same as burning flesh. Cord realized his flesh

was burning as the belt slipped, leaving an exposed area on his thumb.

"Damn! What the hell is that?" Bennet yelled as the first cone landed.

Cord pitched the burning cones toward Bennet's rock fortress. "What the hell is going on?" the sharpshooter yelled. After a dozen cones, Bennet's head popped from behind the rocks like a rattler coming out of its burrow for a nightly feed. He snapped off a quick rifle shot that thudded harmlessly into a pine tree. Cord couldn't return the fire because both his hands were occupied with the cones.

Bennet dropped down and appeared a second later, his British navy Colt in his hand. Cord tossed another fiery cone and the sharpshooter blasted it out of the air as if he was still on stage with Cody's show.

"This is a turkey shoot." The marksman laughed. "Keep 'em coming."

Cord unwound the belt from his hand. He drew his Smith and Wesson and carefully inched his body toward the edge of the tree trunk, hoping for one clear shot at Bennet. The sharpshooter picked up Cord's movement and blasted two quick shots that careened off the pine inches from Cord's face. Cord felt tiny stings like needle punctures as bark chips pelted his cheeks.

Bennet poured more shots in rapid fire, outlining Cord's pine in a barrage of bullets. I've got him spooked, Cord thought, he's making sawdust. Cord moved backward slowly, centering his body behind the protective cover of the tree trunk. He felt a sharp blow as if he had been kicked in the foot and his left leg went out from under him. Cord skidded to the ground, landing on the seat of his pants. The Smith and Wesson flew out of his hand, coming to rest out in the open a few tantalizing feet away.

What the hell happened? Cord knew he wasn't shot. He inspected his foot. Bennet had shot the heel off his boot! When stepping backward he must have exposed it. The sonofabitch is toying with me, Cord thought.

How to get back his revolver? He knew if he stuck out his hand to retrieve it, Snake Eyes could blast off his fingers one by one. Wonderful, he thought. Pinned down and now he had no weapon against the sharpshooter's rifles and pistols. His safe sanctuary had become a prison from which he couldn't escape.

Bennet must be able to see the Smith and Wesson, but he couldn't know that Cord didn't have another gun. My only chance is waiting until dark and slipping away, he thought. Would Bennet wait that long before trying anything?

Cord heard a bullet slice through the air as it whizzed past his ear. The slug had come from the opposite direction of Bennet's position. How the hell did he manage that? Nobody, not even Snake Eyes, could shoot around corners. Bennet's navy Colt spit out four more shots. Cord heard the bullets whine off the boulder behind him. He saw tiny puffs of granite as the slugs chipped away rock and realized what was happening. The trick-shot artist was playing carom shots! A bullet ricocheted off the boulder and burrowed into the ground about six inches from Cord's knee.

"One of them billiard shots is going to put a hole in you, Diamondback," Bennet called down. "I'm getting the angles down. Another dozen rounds or so, and I'll be able to draw a heart on your side of the tree. Why don't you make a grab for that revolver you dropped? I'll hold my fire until your hand is on the gun."

"I threw that one away," Cord said. "My inventory was too big."

"Then why don't I hear some pistol shots?" Bennet asked. "That's your only weapon lying out there."

"If you believe that, come on down and take an open shot at me," Cord said.

"This is more fun," Bennet said. "Killing was getting too easy anyway. At least this has put some of the sport back into it."

The sharpshooter resumed his fusillade, sending a hail of deflected slugs toward Cord's position. More bullets whined into the bark near Cord's head. Snake Eyes alternated using the navy Colt and the repeating Remington so neither weapon got too hot. He was obviously keeping the single shot Winchester loaded and ready in case Cord broke from cover.

A slug ripped through Cord's pants, creasing his thigh like a hiss from a branding iron. Bennet did seem to have zeroed in. Cord knew that sooner or later one of the carom shots would get him. He couldn't stay where he was and do nothing. Careful not to let any part of his arm protrude, he reached toward his pistol with one of the sticks he had used to push the pine cones out of the fire. Maybe he could pull the gun in. Bennet's Remington exploded and Cord's hand jolted, sending shock waves clear to his shoulder, and the stick disintegrated. He pulled back a jagged stump less than three inches long.

"Go out and get the gun yourself," Bennet said. "But don't worry. I could blast it away, but I'm going to leave it there in case you want to try again."

Cord knew you never won if you played the other man's game. Bennet wanted him to try for the Smith and Wesson. Even if he reached it, he couldn't outshoot Snake Eyes. His only weapons were flaming pine cones. Some weapons. Snake Eyes could shoot them out of the air. Even if the cones landed, they were nothing more than a minor annoyance.

Cord looked downhill toward the line cabin. With Anna gone, Jorge dead and Parsons unconscious, no one was in there now. But *something* was probably still there. Something that Bennet cared about very much. Cord rewound the belt around his right hand and pitched a flaming cone toward the cabin. The cone landed five feet from the cabin door and burned itself out. He tried again, this time the cone bounced harmlessly off the the wooden wall.

"You're aiming in the wrong direction." Bennet laughed. "I'm over this way."

Cord pitched six more pine cones in rapid succession. Heat scorched through the leather belt until his hand felt like he had held it over an open flame. On his last two tries, the cones bounced inside the open cabin door. Soon a thin trickle of smoke drifted from the cabin.

"Let the damn thing burn," Bennet said. "What the hell do I care about Parsons' cabin? You probably killed him anyway."

"Where's your supply of laudanum, Bennet?" Cord taunted. "Did you leave it in the cabin for Anna to watch? Is the stuff still there on the table?"

Smoke poured out the door in a single gray column. Flames were visible from the window. The inside of the cabin glowed with a rosy light.

"You bastard," Bennet shouted. "I can't get more until I get back to Denver."

"Why don't you go for the cabin?" Cord asked. "I'll give you the same promise you offered me. And I'm just as sincere as you were."

Six slugs in rapid succession bit into Cord's side of the tree. Bennet had never fired so quickly or carelessly before. He realizes what's happening, Cord thought. Fear must be nibbling at the corners of his mind like a rat eating a trail of grain leading to the main storehouse. The drug must be finally wearing off!

Bennet broke from cover, running straight toward the cabin in a peculiar scuttling form, almost sideways, like a fiddler crab. He held the navy Colt loosely in one hand like a racing baton that would be passed along to another runner. The cabin door was his finish line.

Cord Diamondback arose from his flattened

position. When Bennet started shooting, he had pressed his body to the ground. He retrieved the Smith and Wesson. The gun metal felt cool against his blistered hand. He stood erect, almost at attention, and braced his right arm against the pine-tree trunk. He sighted the barrel of the revolver, leading Bennet slightly, allowing for his downhill speed. Cord squeezed the trigger, steeling himself against the pain when the gun recoiled.

The .44 slug crashed into Bennet's upper chest, shattering his breast plate like a cheap dish. His legs kept pumping downhill, propelled by inertia. He staggered and swayed like a tightrope walker trying to keep his balance.

Cord's gun barrel followed the staggering figure. The revolver jumped a second time and his second shot hit Bennet's rib cage, breaking his third rib and puncturing his left lung.

Bennet's chest pumped hard to draw in air. His thin nostrils flared as he struggled for oxygen. He pitched forward on his head, his body performing an awkward somersault. He flopped on his back in the clearing.

Cord came down to the clearing to inspect the fallen sharpshooter. Bennet's yellow eyes, still flat, watery and filled with glittering evil, looked down at his wounds. The blood flowed out of his body dark and heavy, like a syrup that had been thickened too much. He looked like any other dying man as his hands covered the holes in his chest in a vain effort to stop the flow.

"Lousy shot spread," he coughed, looking up at Cord. His legs twitched involuntarily, making his boots scratch tiny lines in the dirt, like the marks of a ferret. Not a snake after all, Cord thought, just a desperate little animal. "If I had done the shooting, both slugs would have split your heart less than an inch apart." He tilted his head toward the cabin, which was now fully ablaze. "Fireman, fireman, save my child," he said, inexplicably. His blood oozed out of both wounds like slowly moving molasses. He turned to Cord. "Damn Cody and damn you," he whispered. His last curse finished, Bennet closed his yellow snake eyes and died.

21

Charley looked hungrily toward Lafe Parsons, who was tied up like one of his dogies waiting to be branded. "I know I said we'd deal for the man responsible for the ambushings," the miner said. "But your asking price is too high. If I was to agree to take down our dams, the men would lynch me. Without water, we might as well break up camp and go home."

"What happens to the water after it goes through your Long Toms?" Cord asked.

Charley shrugged. "Runs off and soaks into the ground, I guess."

"Then my fee for bringing Lafe Parsons to justice is asking you miners to do what you do best, and that's to dig." Cord scratched a line in the dirt. "I want you to dig another flume leading from your sluice boxes back to the stream bed. After you're finished washing your gravel, the water will find it's old course and flow right back into the valley."

"That's three or four weeks' digging!" Charley said, indignantly. "You're asking the boys to leave their claims for quite a spell."

"Three or four weeks isn't much of a price for peace," Cord said. The miners will get other benefits. You'll be able to go down to the valley for provisions, maybe even a good time. And there's an added bonus."

"Yeah, what's that?" Charley asked suspiciously.

"Gretchen Kreitner won't be back here with more dynamite."

Charley snorted a laugh that shook his gaunt frame. "I forgot about her. Okay, Diamondback, you got a deal. Leave Parsons with us and we'll dig the flume."

Cord shook his head. "I can't do that," he said. "Parsons goes back to Denver with me. He has some testifying to do. Other people are involved. Don't you want them to pay?"

Charley's face turned grim. "He stays here, or we don't dig," he said firmly. "You got the sniper and you got Parsons. I don't give a damn about anybody else, and I'm not taking a chance on some fancy Denver lawyer letting Parsons go free. Besides we want to teach him about coyoting."

Parsons listened to the conversation, a look of terror in his beefy face. A kerchief knotted into his mouth and tied around the back of his head made it impossible for him to speak. Cord had grown tired of his pleading as they approached the mining camp. Parsons' groans were eloquent pleas not to be left with the miners.

Cord realized he had risked the possibility of the miners not giving up Parsons when he brought the rancher into their camp. The killing of Snake Eyes wasn't enough for them. They wanted to see blood. But Parsons was the only living witness against Anna Mellard. Cord weighed the value of bringing her to justice against the value of bringing water to Sheltered Valley. What was revenge worth?

Cord released the reins of Parsons' horse, tugged his own horse around and started out of the camp alone.

Parsons' frantic grunts were quickly drowned out by the yelps of the miners as they closed around him.

22

Three days later Cord had a comfortable, settled in look as he stretched out in Gretchen Kreitner's bed. His left shoulder was elaborately bandaged and Gretchen fed him vegetable soup.

Gretchen's daughters, preteenagers with the same blond hair and blue eyes of their mother, watched from the doorway. Their faces had a solemn look as if spoon-feeding soup was a serious business.

"You say the miners will be sending water down in less than a month?" Gretchen marveled. "That's wonderful, but how did you do it?"

"I had something they wanted to trade," Cord said. "As usual there's a price. I don't know if the railroad will be coming this way. I'm going to Denver to find out."

Gretchen patted the comforter near Cord's hand. She was careful to restrain her obvious affection for him when her children were present. "Why don't you stay here with us?" she asked. "I've talked to the other farmers and ranchers. We're going to dig more wells and the miners' decision will help. With Lafe Parsons out of the way, we'll find a way to share the water."

Cord looked at the beautiful woman standing over him and her daughters peeking at him from the doorway. Living here, making them his family, would be wonderful—but not for long. There was no place he could stay for long. No place where the secret of Christopher Deacon wouldn't seek him out. In a few days he had to return to Denver to collect his five thousand dollars. He'd earned the money. The valley was quiet.

"This will be a nice place to live, Cord," Gretchen continued. She openly caressed his cheek.

Cord said nothing. He thought about the moment when he'd have to tell Jay Mellard that his mother conspired in murder. Would the young tycoon believe him? Probably not. Anna had been back long enough to concoct her own story—no doubt with Cord Diamondback as the villain. She'd be prepared for him, perhaps with newly recruited assassins. What would young Jay Mellard do when he heard Cord's story and listened to his mother's version? Probably react with anger. Cord knew there might be two powerful enemies waiting for him in Denver. But he'd collect his fee and he'd settle with Anna Mellard—one way or the other.

"The girls are staying with a neighbor tonight," Gretchen told Cord. She blushed when she said it.

"Does that mean I sleep in the chicken coop?" Cord asked. "The barn hasn't been rebuilt yet."

"Of course not! You're a wounded man. I couldn't put you out in the cold." She looked at him tenderly. "I know you'll be gone as soon as your wounds heal, but it doesn't matter."

Cord realized that Gretchen was telling him she wanted him on his terms. She bent over to wipe his forehead and Cord smelled the sweet natural perfume of her body. He thought of the problems that awaited him in Denver. He knew he had to go back. In a few days.